FAIRHOPE PUBLIC LIBRARY
007999

The Man on the Bench in the Barn

Georges Simenon

THE MAN ON THE BENCH IN THE BARN

Translated by Moura Budberg

A Helen and Kurt Wolff Book

Harcourt, Brace & World, Inc., New York

ISBN 0-15-156928-2
Library of Congress Catalog Card Number: 73-78875
Printed in the United States of America

B.4.70

Originally published in France under the title *La Main*

Part One

I

I was sitting on the bench in the old barn. Not only was I conscious of being there, staring at the door which was off its hinges and which, with every bang back and forth, let in a great blast of wind and snow, but I saw myself as clearly as in a mirror and was perfectly aware of the incongruity of my situation.

It was an old garden bench painted red. We had three of them, which we used to put away for the winter, along with the lawn mower, the garden tools, and the screens. The barn, a frame one, and also painted red, had been a real barn about a hundred years ago but now was merely a large storehouse. If I start from that particular moment, it is because it was a sort of awakening. I had not slept. Nevertheless, it was as if I had suddenly awakened to reality. Or was a new kind of reality beginning for me just then?

But if that is what it was when does a man begin to . . . No, I refuse to let myself slip along that slope. I'm a lawyer by profession, and it is commonly believed that I'm possessed with a mania of precision.

In fact, I did not even have any idea of what time it was. Two in the morning? Maybe three?

At my feet, on the beaten earth floor, the pink filaments of the small flashlight glowed gently but gave no light at all. My fingers were numb from the cold, and I tried to strike a match to light my cigarette. I wanted to smoke. It was like a sign of recovered reality. The smell of tobacco seemed to reassure me and I remained there, leaning forward, my elbows on my knees, staring at the great door that banged back and forth and which any minute now would probably collapse under the pressure of the blizzard.

I had been drunk. I was probably still drunk, and it had only happened to me twice before. In spite of that, I remembered everything the way you remember a dream, piecing it together bit by bit.

The Sanderses had come to spend the weekend with us, on their return from a trip to Canada. Ray is one of my oldest friends. We both went to law school at Yale and later, after we both had married, we continued to see one another.

So far, so good. That evening, Saturday, January 15th, with the snow already falling, I asked Ray:

"Would it bore you to come along for a drink over at old Ashbridge's?"

"Harold Ashbridge, from Boston?"

"Yes."

"I thought he spent the winter at his place in Florida."

"He bought an estate twenty miles from here about ten years ago; he likes to play the gentleman farmer.

He always spends Christmas and the New Year there. Then he gives an enormous party and departs for Florida about the middle of January."

Ashbridge is one of the few people who impress me. Ray is another one. When I come to think of it, they are not as few as all that. Even without counting the women. For instance there's Mona, Ray's wife—I always treat her as a small exotic animal, though as far as exoticism goes she has just a quarter of Italian blood in her veins.

"He doesn't know me."

"No one needs to know anyone at Ashbridge's."

Isabel listened without saying a word. She never interferes on these occasions. She is the very picture of the tactful woman. She never objects. She is quite content to observe and to pass judgment.

At that moment my behavior provided no grounds for criticism. We go to the party at Ashbridge's every year; it has become a professional obligation. She made no comment on the fact that it was snowing hard and that the road to North Hillsdale wasn't a good one.

"Which car shall we take?"

I said:

"Let's take mine."

And though it is only now that I realize it, there was a hidden motive in my answer. Ray works on Madison Avenue. He's one of the partners in one of the largest public-relations organizations. We see each other almost every time I go to New York, and I know his habits.

Without being an alcoholic, he needs two or three

double Martinis before every meal, like almost all the people in his profession who live on their nerves. He might easily drink a bit too much at Ashbridge's.

It is comic, or tragic, to remember these small details a few hours later. Afraid that Ray might have one drink too many, I was making sure I was the one to drive on the way back. While in fact it was I who got drunk.

There were at least fifty guests when we got there, if not more. A huge buffet supper was spread out on a table in the hall, all the doors were open, and people were coming and going on the first floor and there were bottles and glasses everywhere.

"Mrs. Ashbridge, Mrs. Sanders—Patricia . . . my friend Ray . . ."

Patricia is only thirty. She is Ashbridge's third wife. She is a very handsome woman. Not as handsome as . . . I shouldn't say as Isabel, for my wife has never been really handsome. . . . Besides, I have always found it difficult to describe women, and automatically I do it by comparing them with my wife.

Isabel is tall, her figure is well proportioned, she has regular features, a slightly condescending smile, as though the person she is addressing has done something that requires forgiveness.

Patricia is just about the exact opposite. Petite, somewhat like Mona. With an even darker complexion than Mona's, but with green eyes. She looks at you as if you fascinated her, she really does, as if she wanted nothing more than to penetrate your secret life and to open hers to you.

Isabel never makes you think of a bedroom. Patricia, on the other hand, always makes you see a bed. . . .

There have been rumors. . . . But I am not concerned with rumors. In the first place, I usually disbelieve them. Then I have an instinctive horror of indiscretion and even more so of slander.

The Russells were there, the Dyers, the Collinses, the Greens, the Hassbergers, the . . .

"Hello, Ted. . . ."

"Hello, Dan. . . ."

There was talking and drinking and milling about, and then nibbling at all those little tidbits that taste of fish or turkey or meat. I remember having a serious conversation, in the corner of the small living room, with Bill Hassberger, who is planning to send me to Chicago to settle a matter of litigation.

These people are rich. One wonders why they live for the greater part of the year in our little corner of Connecticut, but they have interests and connections in the neighborhood.

By comparison I'm a poor man. So is Dr. Warren, with whom I exchanged a few words. I wasn't drunk, far from it. I cannot say at what precise moment that began. Or rather I've just noticed it now, in the last few seconds, for I've suddenly become aware of a curious lucidity, sitting here on my bench and smoking at least my fifth cigarette in succession.

I had gone upstairs aimlessly, like many of the other guests before and after me. I had pushed open a door and quickly closed it again, but not before I had time to see

Ray and Patricia. The room wasn't even a room, it was a bathroom and they were making love in it, in their clothes.

I may be forty-five years of age, but this picture struck me so forcefully that I can re-create it again in all its details. I'm sure that Patricia saw me. I'm even sure that it wasn't embarrassment that flickered in her eyes but a kind of amused challenge. That is very important. That picture is of considerable importance for me. Sitting on my bench in the barn, I could only get a glimpse of it, but later I had all the time to turn it over in my mind.

I'm not trying to make out that this was my reason for taking to the bottle, but nevertheless it was about that time that I began to empty all the glasses that came within my reach. Isabel caught me at it and I blushed, of course.

"It's so hot," I muttered.

She didn't warn me. In fact she said nothing. She merely smiled the terrible smile that forgives or that . . . Or that what? That'll come later. I'm not there yet. There are so many other things that must be explained.

One summer I took it upon myself to clear out the barn, intending to sort everything, to throw some things away and store those that were to be kept. After a few hours I was exhausted, and hadn't the courage to go on.

I was reminded of it when I made another inventory that night on the red bench in that same barn, but this time I would not give up halfway through. I'd finish the job, whatever the cost and whatever I discovered.

There was the picture of Ray and Patricia to fit into

place. Then, at a certain moment, old Ashbridge's glance. He's not an alcoholic either, but a man who likes a drink, particularly after five o'clock in the afternoon. He is fat, but not too fat, and his round light eyes are always moist.

"Well, Donald?"

We were both not far from the table, with several noisy groups around us. There were many conversations going on at once—overlapping, blending.

Why did I have the impression that we were suddenly isolated, he and I? Confronted would be the more correct way of putting it. For it was barely five minutes after the scene in the bathroom. He was looking at me calmly, but he was looking at me. I know very well what I am talking about. Most of the time, especially at such parties, you don't look at the person you are talking to. You know he is there. You talk. You listen. You answer. You let your eyes glide over a face, over a shoulder. . . .

He was looking at me, and the two words he had just pronounced seemed like a deliberate question.

"Well, Donald?"

What did he mean by "well"? Had he also witnessed the scene? And did he know that I had witnessed it?

He didn't appear depressed or menacing. But he wasn't smiling either. Was he jealous? Did he know that Patricia was in the habit of . . . It was I who felt guilty, as he went on.

"Your friend Sanders is a remarkable fellow."

Some of the guests were leaving. One could see them in the hall putting on their coats, pulling on their rubbers, which had been lined up on a shelf. Every time the door opened and closed, a sharp icy blast of air rushed in.

Then there was the sound of the wind, monotonous at first, then growing more powerful, and the guests began to look at each other inquiringly.

"Is it still snowing?"

"Yes."

"That means we're in for a blizzard."

Why I went on drinking, entirely contrary to my habit, I cannot understand to this moment. I went from one group to the other and familiar faces took on a new aspect in my eyes. I believe that at a particular moment I laughed sneeringly at someone and Isabel caught me at it.

There was a certain tension in the air; most of the guests had quite a distance to go; some lived in New York State, others in Massachusetts, and had a drive of forty miles ahead of them.

I was one of the last to leave. I heard the sound of voices and exclamations every time a group left the house and was met by an increasingly violent wind that seemed to penetrate every corner.

"In an hour the snow will be two feet high."

I don't know who said that. Then Isabel took my arm, in the natural manner of a good wife, without any affectation. I realized that it was time for us to go, too.

"Where is Mona?"

"She went to get her coat in Pat's room."

"And Ray?"

Ray was beside me, the everyday Ray, the Ray I had known for over twenty-five years.

"Are we going?" he asked.

"Yes, I guess so."

"Evidently you can't see what's right in front of you."

I did not shake Patricia's hand as I always do. I admit that I made a show of it, that it gave me a dubious pleasure. I wonder . . . did old Ashbridge notice?

"Let's get going, kids."

There were only three or four cars left in front of the house. We had to walk bent almost double, the wind was so powerful, hitting us in the face with hard snow particles. The two women sat in the back. I took the wheel, Isabel making no comment as to whether or not I was in a fit condition to drive. I wasn't depressed, despondent, or tired either. On the contrary, I was pleasantly exhilarated and the noise and the storm made me want to sing.

"That's one over with!"

"One of what?"

"One of the parties. . . . There's one more to get through next week, at the Russells', and then we'll be left in peace until spring."

From time to time the windshield wipers stuck and hesitated before starting up again. The snow swept almost horizontal white streaks in front of the headlights. I let myself be guided by the dark line of trees, for there was no seeing the borders of the road.

Behind me, in the warmth of the car and the furs, I could hear the two women making ordinary conversation.

"You weren't too bored, Mona?"

"Not at all. Patricia's charming. In fact everybody was very nice."

"In three days they'll be in Florida."

"Ray and I thought we might go for a few days to Miami next month."

I had to lean forward and peer in front of me, and several times I had to get out of the car to scrape the ice off the windshield. The third time the strength of the wind almost pushed me off my feet.

We have several of these storms every winter, and they're usually fairly severe. We know all the difficult places by now, all the ditches and roads to avoid.

Which way did we have to take to get back to Brentwood? Did we go by Copake or Great Barrington? I couldn't tell you now. "It's really a beauty, Ray," I remember saying. The perfect snowstorm. A blizzard, in fact. When I turned on the radio, that was the word they used. They spoke of gusts of more than sixty miles an hour around Albany and hundreds of cars blocked on the roads to the north.

Instead of making me tense and anxious, this stimulated me, as if I were welcoming with a great surge of relief something exceptional that was happening in my life.

We spoke little, Ray and I. He looked ahead, frowning when visibility became almost nil. Then, as if on purpose, I drove faster.

I had no ax to grind with him. He was my friend. He had done me no harm by making love with Patricia Ashbridge. I wasn't in love with her. I wasn't in love with any woman, I was content with Isabel. What could I possibly have had against him?

I had to maneuver for some minutes because of a snowdrift, and I used one of the bags of sand that we always keep in the trunk in the winter. I had snow in my eyes, my nose, and my ears, and it even penetrated the seams of my clothes.

"Where are we?"

"We've got another three miles to go."

It had become more and more difficult to move at all. We met three snowplows, but the snow formed a solid mass again as soon as they passed and there was no longer a question of using the windshield wipers. I had to get out all the time, to scrape away the ice.

"Are we staying on the road?"

Isabel's voice was calm. She was merely asking a question, nothing more.

"I should hope so!" I replied gaily.

Actually, I no longer knew. It was only when we crossed the small stone bridge about a mile away from home that I was able to get my bearings. But on the other side of the bridge the snow had formed a wall and the front of the car went straight into it and got stuck.

"Last stop, kids. Everybody out."

"What do you mean?"

"Everybody out. . . . The Chrysler's not a bulldozer, you know. We're going to have to walk."

Ray looked at me, wondering if I was serious. Isabel

had understood, because it had happened to us twice before.

"Will you take the flashlight?"

I fished it out of the glove compartment and turned it on. We had not used it for months, and, as might have been expected, it gave out a fairly weak yellow glimmer.

"Well, here we go!"

At that moment it was all still quite gay. I can see the women arm in arm, diving into the snow in front of us. I followed with the flashlight and Ray walked beside me saying nothing. Nobody spoke, in fact. It was hard enough to breathe in the blizzard without wasting any more effort.

Isabel fell and bravely got back onto her feet. From time to time both women disappeared in the darkness. I called out, my hand covering my mouth to keep out the icy air:

"Hi, there! Hi!"

And a faint "Hi" came back at me. The light from the flashlight grew fainter and fainter. Suddenly, when we were about three hundred yards away from the house, it died completely.

"Hi, there!"

"Hi. . . ."

I must have been very close to the women, because I could hear their feet crunching through the snow. I could also hear Ray's footsteps somewhere to my right. I was beginning to feel giddy. The energy provided by the alcohol was seeping away and I moved with increasing difficulty. I felt a pain in the chest where the heart is, or so it seemed to me, and I became anxious. Hadn't men of my age, even in prime condition, died from heart failure under circumstances like these?

"Hi, there!"

My head reeled. I could hardly lift my feet. I could see nothing. All I could hear was the deafening clamor of the blizzard and I was covered with snow.

I don't know how long it went on. I was no longer concerned with the others. I was still holding the useless flashlight in my hand like an idiot and had to stop every two or three steps to get my breath back.

At last there was a wall, and a door that opened in it.

"Come in. . . ."

A burst of warm air came from the darkness of the house.

"Where's Ray?"

I was bewildered. I wondered why the women hadn't turned the lights on. I stretched my hand out to the switch.

"There's no current. . . . Where's Ray?"

"He was right beside me. . . ."

I went to the front door and called out:

"Ray! . . . Ray! . . . Where are you?"

I seemed to hear a voice, but it is easy enough to hear voices in a blizzard.

"Ray!"

"Get the flashlight from the night table."

We keep another flashlight on our night table, because from time to time there are power failures. I groped my way through the rooms, bumping against furniture that I did not recognize. Then there was a light behind me coming from one of the red candles in the dining room.

It was strange to see Isabel appearing faintly in the darkness bearing a silver candlestick.

"You've found it?"

"Yes. . . ."

I held the flashlight in my hand but it gave almost as little light as the one in the car.

"Where are the batteries?"

"You didn't see any in the drawer?"

"No. . . ."

I needed a drink to pull me together, but I did not dare take one. The women said nothing. They weren't pushing me to it, but I got the distinct impression that they were sending me, armed with a semiextinct flashlight, out into the blizzard, to look for Ray.

I'll leave out nothing, otherwise I might as well never have begun. One thing I must make clear: at no point in the evening had I really been stone drunk.

If I try to describe my condition as precisely as possible, I would say that I was in the grip of a kind of perverse lucidity. Reality was there all around me and I was part of it. I was aware of everything I did and had done. With a pencil and paper I could probably have given a fairly accurate list of every word I had uttered, starting at the Ashbridges', then in the car, and then at home.

But on my bench where I sat shaking with cold, lighting one cigarette after another, I felt as if I was beginning to reach a new kind of clarity that disturbed me and was beginning to be more terrifying every minute. It consisted of a word, or rather of three words, which I imagined I could hear over and over again:

"You killed him."

Perhaps not in the legal sense. And I'm not even sure of that. Withholding of assistance to a person in danger is surely synonymous with murder.

When I walked out of the house after the two women had sent me to look for Ray, I turned at once to the right. To be accurate, in order to delude them, in case they were watching me through the window and could see the glimmer of my flashlight, I walked straight ahead for about a hundred feet; then I turned to the right in the security of the darkness, knowing that I would find the barn about thirty feet away.

I was physically exhausted. I was morally exhausted too. This fantastic storm, this natural phenomenon that only recently had stimulated me to the point of intense nervous excitement, suddenly filled me with terror.

Why had the others stayed at home? Why hadn't they come out to look with me? I could see Isabel, serene as a statue, holding the silver candlestick up above her shoulder. Mona's features seemed blurred in the obscurity, but she hadn't said a word. Neither of them seemed to understand that this was a tragedy and that in sending me out they were exposing me to danger as well. My heart was pounding, I was gasping for breath all the time.

I was afraid, I've already said so. I called out again once or twice:

"Ray!"

It would have been a miracle if he'd heard me or indeed

seen the faint flicker of my flashlight in a fall of snow that was almost parallel to the ground. It was not falling, it was whipping against me, great fistfuls of it beating at my face, half stifling me.

I heard the barn door squeak and rushed into it, flinging myself down on a bench.

A red bench. A garden bench. I realized a certain grotesque quality in the situation: a man of forty-five, a lawyer and a respectable citizen, sitting on a red bench and lighting his first cigarette with trembling fingers as if it were going to warm his whole body, in the middle of the night, in a blizzard. . . .

"I killed him!"

Not yet, maybe. He was probably still alive but dying, within minutes of death. He didn't know the lie of the land as I did, and if he had turned to the right, even for a few yards, he would stumble from the steep rock down to the ice-covered stream.

The thought left me unmoved. I hadn't the courage to go and look for him, to take any risks. Quite the opposite.

And it all amounts to the same thing . . . it all points to that one conclusion that I've had to come to: that, in fact, I came to, little by little, that night of January 15th and 16th as I sat on my bench in the barn. For what was happening now to Ray did not really distress me.

Would I have been in the same frame of mind if I'd not been drinking at the Ashbridges'? It's not easy to say and actually it doesn't change much. Would I have felt the same perverse relief had I not pushed open the door into the bathroom and caught Ray making love to Patricia?

Seen from there, it looks different. I'm getting very close to the solid core of my ruminations. For it was ruminations more than consecutive thoughts that I was indulging in as I sat there on my bench.

I had plenty of time. I was supposed to be searching for Ray. The longer I stayed away, the more grateful they would be to me.

What Ray was doing that evening in the bathroom with a woman he'd barely known two hours ago, beautiful and desirable Patricia, I had dreamed a hundred, a thousand times, of doing myself.

He married Mona, who, like Patricia, makes one think of bed.

And I—I had married Isabel.

That's all there is to it.

But it isn't all. I had started, God knows why, to examine just a part of the everyday truth, to see myself in a different kind of mirror, and now the whole fabric of the old truth that had become more or less a habit was disintegrating, bit by bit.

It dated back to Yale. No, it went back further than Yale, before I ever knew Ray. It went back, in fact, to my childhood. How I longed . . . If only I could find the right words! How I longed to do things, to be somebody, to take risks, to look people straight in the eye and tell them . . .

Yes, to look at people as old Ashbridge looked at them for instance; a short time ago he had made me feel like a small boy. He didn't take the trouble to speak, to assume an attitude. He wasn't trying to communicate. We stood face to face. Perhaps he was seeing through the deep recesses of my head? I was a creature of no importance.

He was seventy and had never been a handsome man. He tossed off those drinks of his, which gave his eyes that slightly vacant look, and dozens of visitors invaded his home. Did he care what they thought about him? He provided them with food and drink, with chairs and open rooms, including the bathroom where Patricia . . .

Was he aware that his wife was unfaithful to him? Did it hurt him? Or, on the contrary, did he despise poor Ray, who was one of many and who, in five minutes, would have lost all importance, had already lost all importance, and who probably that same night would be succeeded by someone else in one of the other rooms or even in the same room?

I admired Ashbridge, and not only because he was rich and had interests in some fifty different concerns, from shipping to television.

When he had settled in the neighborhood ten years ago, I would have liked him to be my client if only to be concerned with a small part of his affairs.

"I must talk to you one of these days," he had said to me.

The years passed and he had never talked to me. I bore him no grudge.

With Ray it was different, because he and I were the same age, almost of the same background, and had had the same education. At Yale I was the more brilliant pupil; now he had become an important figure on Madison Avenue, while I was merely a respectable little lawyer in Brentwood, Connecticut.

Ray was taller than I was, stronger, too. Even at the age of twenty he could look at people the way old Ashbridge did. I've met many men like that. Some of my clients, for example. My attitude toward them alters according to circumstances and my state of mind. Sometimes I think it's been admiration, at others I must confess to a certain envy.

And now, I knew, sitting on my bench, I knew that it was hate.

They frightened me. They were too strong for me or else it was I who was too weak for them. I can remember the evening Ray introduced me to Mona. She was wearing a little black silk dress and beneath it every hidden patch of her body was vibrating with life.

Why not for me?

Isabel for me. Mona for him.

And if I chose Isabel, it was, wasn't it, precisely because I had never dared approach a Mona, or a Patricia, or any of the women whom I had once desired to the point of clenching my fists in fury and frustration?

The wind blew with such violence that I expected at any moment to see the roof of the barn fly off. The top hinge of the door was broken and it was hanging sideways, which didn't prevent it from knocking against the wall. The snow forced its way in and reached my feet. I went on thinking in a kind of trance, a kind of lucid delirium.

"I killed you, Ray. . . ."

And what if I said it to them, to the two women sitting in the warm house lit up by a candle?

They wouldn't have believed me, I wasn't the kind of man to kill Ray, or anybody else, for that matter.

Nevertheless, I had done it, and the knowledge gave me a vague, heady pleasure, as if I had just helped myself to a strong drink.

I rose to my feet. Surely they wouldn't expect me to stay outside for hours. Also I was numb with cold and was worried about my heart. I have always been afraid that my heart would suddenly stop beating.

I dived into the snow, which beat at my face, my chest, and wrapped around my legs. I had to struggle to pull out one leg, then the other.

"Ray!"

I had to make sure not to make a mistake, not to move away from the road. I couldn't see the house. I had taken my bearings when I left the barn. Now all I had to do was to walk in a straight line.

And what if I found Ray with the two women in front of the fire in the living room? I could imagine them, watching me coming in like a ghost and saying with a smile:

"Where have you been all that time?"

This frightened me so much that I found the strength to walk more quickly, so that I bumped against the wall of the house and began to grope for the door. They hadn't heard me as I came nearer. I turned the handle and the first thing I saw were the logs burning in the fireplace, then someone in an armchair wearing Isabel's light blue dressing gown. It wasn't Isabel. It was Mona.

"Where is she?"

"Isabel? She went to prepare some food. But, Donald!"

It was almost a scream.

"Donald!"

She did not rise from her chair. She didn't look at me. She stared at the flames in the fireplace. Her face reflected no feeling, she looked stunned.

She added very softly:

"You haven't found him?"

"No."

"You were away so long. . . ."

Yes, some time had passed and she had begun to realize . . .

"He is very strong, you know," I said. "Much stronger than I am. . . . Perhaps he's got . . ."

"Perhaps what?"

How could I lie? And how could Ray have found his way in this ocean of snow and ice?

Isabel came in, carrying the candlestick in one hand, a plate of sandwiches in the other. She looked at me and went pale. Her face was rigid. . . .

"Eat, Mona. . . ."

How long does it take to die, buried in the snow? Another three, four hours, and then dawn would come.

"Did you try to telephone?" I asked.

"All the lines are dead."

She pointed with her eyes to a small transistor.

"We've been getting the news every quarter of an hour. . . . Apparently the storm has spread from the Canadian border to New York. The electricity and the telephones are out. . . ."

She added automatically:

"Ray should have held on to your arm, the way we both did with each other."

"He was walking on my right, quite close to me."

Mona didn't weep. She held a sandwich in her hand and finally bit into it.

"Is there anything to drink, Isabel?"

"Beer? Liquor? I can't fix anything hot, because the stove is electric."

"Is there any whisky?"

"You should also have a bath, Donald. Later on, there won't be any hot water."

It is true that the heater gets switched off. Everything is electric, even the clocks, except the little one in our bedroom. I understood now why Mona was wearing one of Isabel's dressing gowns. My wife had made her have a bath, to get her relaxed as much as to warm her up.

"Did you go to the car?"

"Yes. . . ."

Again I was overcome with fear. What if Ray had in fact found himself near the car as he zigzagged in the snow? In that case the wisest thing would have been to get into it and wrap himself up as best he could and wait for morning.

Our house, Yellow Rock Farm, isn't situated on the highway. We have a long private road. The neighbors are at a distance of about a mile. "If I know Ray . . ." my wife murmured.

I was waiting with curiosity for the end of the sentence.

"He'll manage somehow. . . . He'll get out of it."

Not me . . . but he would. Because he's Ray. Because he's not Donald Dodd.

"Aren't you going to have a bath? Take the candle. We'd better save them a bit and just light one at a time. We can manage in here with the light from the fire."

The radiators would be going cold. They were practically cold already. In a few hours there would be no heat anywhere except in the living room. We would have to huddle in it, the three of us, as close as we could get to the fire.

It was my turn to take the candlestick and go to our room. Suddenly I longed for another drink. I turned around and saw Isabel pouring a whisky for Mona.

I took a glass from the cupboard and took the bottle from her. I understood the look my wife gave me. As always, there was no reproach. Not even a silent warning. It was a special kind of look, and I had seen it over and over again through the years, probably ever since we had known each other. In that look lay a whole catalogue of indictments.

She registered, without comment, without judgment, even forbidding herself any judgment. But the facts were there, in ordered columns, one after the other. There must have been millions, billions of them. Seventeen years of life together, not counting one year of engagement.

Deliberately I poured myself the double if not the treble of what I usually drank.

"To your good health, Mona. . . ."

It was a ridiculous toast, but she didn't seem to hear me. I gulped the whisky down. The heat spread through my body and only then did I realize how frozen I had been.

The bathroom reminded me of the one at the Ashbridges' and called up a fantasy the vulgarity of which made me blush with shame:

"At least he had had a last moment of bliss. . . ."

Why was I so sure that Ray was dead? The hypothesis of the car was perfectly reasonable. Maybe Isabel had guessed right. She didn't know, of course, that I hadn't gone as far as that. It was less likely, but he might possibly have reached one of the neighboring houses. . . . Since the telephones were dead, he would not have been able to let us know.

"I killed him. . . ."

Mona thought as I did, she knew he was dead. I had immediately sensed it from her attitude. Did she really love Ray? Were there people who loved each other after many years together?

Ray and Mona had no children. We have two, two girls, who are in one of the best schools in Connecticut, Adams, at Litchfield, run by a Miss Jenkins. Did they have any light at Litchfield?

Mildred is fifteen, Cecilia twelve, and they come home for the weekend once every fortnight. It was just lucky it hadn't been their weekend.

The water was running in the bath. I put my hand to the faucet just in time to notice that it was already cold and I had to be content with a third of a tubful.

It was strange, that night, to realize you were a decent fellow, one of the two partners of the firm of Higgins and Dodd, married, with two daughters, owner of Yellow Rock Farm, one of the oldest and most pleasant houses of Brentwood, and to know that you had killed a man.

By omission, it is true. Having failed to search for him. But who can tell? I could have spent hours with my feeble flashlight wandering in the snow, and still not have found him. In my mind, was it? That was more exact. I hadn't searched. As soon as I was out of sight of the house I had made my way to the barn and sheltered there.

Would Mona be grief-stricken? Did she know that Ray slept with other women whenever he had a chance? Who knows if she wasn't like Patricia herself? Perhaps Ray and Mona were not of a jealous nature, and told each other these adventures. I'd find out somehow. If anyone was going to profit from the situation, it would be me.

I almost dozed off in the tub and had to be careful not to slip as I got out, because I wasn't at all sure of my movements.

What were we going to do, the three of us? There was no question of bed. Can you go to bed if your guest's husband . . . ?

No, we wouldn't go to bed. Besides, the rooms were beginning to be icy and I shuddered in my bathrobe. I chose a pair of gray flannel trousers, and a thick pull-over which I usually only put on to sweep the snow off the paths.

The candle had burned out, and I lit the other one and put my slippers on to go to the living room.

"Do you know if there are any logs left in the cellar?"

We hardly ever used them. We light the fire only when we have friends in the house. You have to go to the cellar through a trap door and down a ladder, which complicated things.

"I believe there are."

I looked automatically at the whisky bottle. When I had left the two women it had been half full. There was only a little of it left at the bottom of the bottle.

Isabel had followed my eyes, obviously, and obviously had understood me.

She also looked at Mona and her glance provided me with the reply. Mona, her face flushed, was asleep in her armchair and the dressing gown revealed a naked knee.

II

When I opened my eyes, I was lying on the sofa in the sitting room and someone had thrown a blue and yellow tartan rug over me. The sun had risen, but the daylight only filtered faintly through the windowpanes, which were covered with a thick layer of hard snow.

What struck me at first, probably what really woke me up, was a familiar smell, the smell of all the ordinary mornings: the smell of coffee. Memories of the evening and the night began to come back. I wondered if the electric power had been restored. Then, turning my head slightly, I saw Isabel on her knees before the fire.

I had a terrible headache, and I hated having to face the realities of another day. I should have liked to go back to sleep, but before I had had time to close my eyes again my wife asked me:

"Have you had a little rest?"

"Yes . . . yes, I think so. . . ."

I got up and realized that I had been more drunk than I'd thought. My whole body ached and I felt giddy.

"You'll get some coffee in a moment. . . ."

"Have you slept?" I asked in my turn.

"I dozed."

But of course she hadn't. She had watched over Mona and me. She had been superb, as she always was. It was in her nature to behave perfectly, whatever the circumstances. I could see her, sitting upright in her armchair, watching us in turn, getting up noiselessly, now and then, to keep the fire alive.

Then, with the first light of dawn, putting out the precious candle, she must have gone to the kitchen to get the pan with the longest handle. While we slept she had thought about the coffee.

"Where is Mona?"

"She went to get dressed. . . ."

In the spare room at the end of the hall where the windows looked out on the pond. I remembered the two blue leather suitcases that Ray had taken there the day before the Ashbridges' party.

"How is she?"

"She doesn't seem to grasp what's happened."

I could hear the noise of the storm, as violent as it had been when I fell asleep. Isabel was pouring coffee into my usual cup, for we both have our special cups; mine is a little larger than hers, because I drink a lot of coffee.

"We'll have to bring up some more logs."

There were none left in the basket to the right of the fireplace, and those that were burning would soon be ashes.

"I'll go in a moment."

"You don't want me to help you?"

"No, thanks. . . ."

I guessed that she had watched me surreptitiously

and realized that I had a hangover. She missed nothing. What was the point of cheating?

I finished my coffee, lit a cigarette, and went into the small room next to the sitting room, which is called the library because one of the walls is covered with books. Lifting the oval carpet, I opened the trap door and only then remembered that I needed a candle.

All this was confused, phantomlike.

"How many candles have we left?"

"Five. I've just got Hartford on the radio."

It is the nearest big town.

"Nearly all the villages are in the same state. The lines are being repaired all over, but they can't get to a lot of the places."

I could picture the men climbing the posts in the blizzard, the snowplows forcing their way through the heavy drifts.

I climbed down the ladder, holding a candle, and went to the back of the cellar, cut into the rock, the yellow rock that had given its name to the old farm. I was tempted to sit down for a while, just to be alone and to think.

But think about what? It was all over. There was nothing to think about. . . .

All I had to do was to bring up the logs.

I remember that morning as something greenish gray, overcast, like some of the Sundays of my childhood when it rained and I was unable to get out and didn't know what to do with myself. It seemed to me then that people and things were not in their right places, that noises were not the same as usual, those of the road as well as those inside. I was in a kind of limbo, and had what I called a sinking feeling.

I was reminded of a ridiculous little detail. Sometimes when my father stayed in bed later than usual I would watch him as he shaved. He would pace up and down in an old dressing gown, and his smell was different too, just as the smell of my parents' room was different perhaps because it was cleaned later than usual in the day.

"Good morning, Donald. . . . Did you manage to get some sleep?"

"Yes, I did, thanks. And you?"

"Well, you know . . ."

She was wearing black slacks and a yellow pullover. Her hair was carefully arranged, she had made up her face; now she was listlessly smoking a cigarette, turning the spoon in her cup.

"What are we going to do?"

She said it because she had to say something, without conviction, watching the flames. . . .

"I think I could fry you some eggs . . . there are some in the icebox."

"I'm not hungry."

"Neither am I. . . . If there's any coffee left . . ."

As far as I was concerned, all I needed was coffee and cigarettes. I went to open the door and had to hold it fast against the wind. I could hardly recognize the outside world. The snow made waves three or four feet high. It was still falling as thick and fast as in the night, and you could only guess at the red shape of the barn.

"Do you think we could try?" Isabel asked me.

Try what? To go in search of Ray?

"I'll put on my boots and my parka. . . ."

"I'll go with you."

"I too."

All this was senseless, and I realized it fully. I longed to tell them quite simply and calmly:

"It is useless to search for Ray. . . . I killed him." For I remembered having killed him. . . . I remembered all that had happened on the bench, all that had gone through my mind. Why did my wife keep looking at me so suspiciously?

She knew I had been drinking, of course. It is not a crime. A man has a right to get drunk once or twice in his life. I had chosen the wrong evening, but how was I to know it?

Besides, it was Ray's fault. If he hadn't dragged Patricia to the bathroom on the first floor . . .

All right, then. I'd go through the motions once again. I put on my boots, put on my parka. Isabel did the same, saying to Mona:

"No, you stay here. Somebody's got to keep the fire going. . . ."

We walked one beside the other, jostling one another in the snow, which rose in front of us as we tried to keep going. . . . I felt giddy and was afraid I'd collapse, exhausted. I didn't want to be the first to give in.

"It's useless . . ." Isabel decided at last.

Before we went back into the house, we scraped one

of the windowpanes, so that we would be able to see something outside. Mona had resumed her place in front of the fire and asked no questions.

She was listening to the radio. From Hartford we heard that roofs had been swept away, that hundreds of cars were stranded on the roads. They mentioned the places that had been hardest hit, but said nothing of Brentwood. . . .

"In any case, we've got to eat."

Having decided this, Isabel went to the kitchen and Mona and I sat next to each other. I wondered if it was perhaps the first time we'd been alone together in a room. I decided it probably was, and it gave me a curious pleasure. . . .

How old was she? Thirty-five? A bit more? She had been on the stage in the past and had appeared on television. Her father was a playwright. He wrote successful musical comedies, and had had a restless life until he had died three or four years ago.

What was the mystery around Mona? None at all. She was a woman like any other. Before marrying Ray, she must have had a few affairs. . . .

"It all seems so unreal to me, Donald. . . ."

I looked at her and was deeply moved. I would have liked to take her in my arms, stroke her hair. Was all this compatible with a Donald Dodd?

"It seems unreal to me, too. . . ."

"You risked your life, last night, going to search for him. . . ."

I was silent. I felt no shame. On the whole, I was enjoying this intimate moment. . . .

"Ray was a good sort," she murmured a little later.

It seemed to me that she spoke of him as of someone already far away, with a kind of detachment. . . .

After a rather long silence, she added: "We got on so well, he and I."

Isabel came in with a pan and eggs.

"It's the easiest thing to prepare. There's some ham in the icebox for anyone who wants it."

She knelt, as she had done this morning, in front of the fire, and managed to balance the pan on the logs.

What were all the other people doing in their houses? Probably much the same. Except that not everyone had a fire and logs. The Ashbridges would have to postpone their trip to Florida.

And the girls, in Adams? Did the school have enough fuel to heat the rooms? I reassured myself with the thought that Litchfield was a biggish place and that there was no news of power failures in the larger towns.

"The most devastating blizzard in sixty-two years . . ."

After the news, the radio went back to music and I turned it off.

We had to keep close to the fire as we ate, because at a distance of ten feet the cold was penetratingly sharp.

Why did Isabel . . . ? All the time we've known one another, as I have already said, she has always looked at me in a particular way, but that morning it seemed to me that there was something different in her expression. At one point I even imagined I understood what the look signified:

"I know."

There was no anger. No trace of accusation. Just a simple statement of fact.

"I know you and I know . . ."

True, my hangover was still there and twice I almost threw up my breakfast. I longed to have a drink, to regain my self-assurance, but I didn't dare.

Why? Questions again. I spend my life asking myself questions, not many, a few, some of them idiotic, and I never find satisfactory answers.

I'm a man, after all. Isabel had found it perfectly normal, last night, to see about fifty men and women well and truly drunk. Well, what I had done was almost to snatch the glasses stealthily and drink them in hiding. Why?

She had been the first to pour some whisky when we came back for Mona, who is a woman, after all, and I had to wait a long time before daring to pour some for myself. What prevented me now from opening the liquor cupboard, taking out a bottle, and getting a glass from the kitchen? I needed it. I was literally shaking. I had no desire to get drunk, just to recover my self-assurance.

It took me more than half an hour, and even then I cheated.

"Wouldn't you like a whisky, Mona?"

She glanced at Isabel, as if asking her approval, as if my offer wasn't sufficient.

"Perhaps it would do me good?"

"And you, Isabel?"

"No, thanks. . . ."

Usually, except for the parties we go to or those that we give at home, I drink one whisky a day when I come back from the office before dinner. Often Isabel takes one with me, a very weak one, I admit.

She isn't a puritan. She doesn't criticize either the people who drink or those of our friends who lead a more or less irregular life.

In that case why such timidity, for heaven's sake? One might think I was afraid of her. But afraid of what, exactly? Of a reproach? She had never reproached me. What was it, then? Was I afraid of that look of hers? Just as, when I was a child, I had been afraid to meet my mother's eyes? Isabel isn't my mother. I'm her husband and we've produced two children together. She never does anything without asking my advice first.

She isn't at all the strong, domineering wife of whom husbands complain, and when we have company she always leaves the last word to me.

She is calm and serene, that's all. Perhaps that last word is the key to the whole thing.

"Your health, Mona. . . ."

"And yours, Donald. . . . And yours, Isabel. . . ."

Mona was not trying to act the inconsolable wife. She may have suffered, but it can't have been a devastating grief. . . . She had said, as from the depths of her heart:

"Ray was a good sort."

Was that not revealing? The kind of thing one would

say of a pal, of a good friend, with whom one had shared a part of one's life in the most pleasant way possible.

This, too, attracted me. I had, long ago, felt between them this peaceful, indulgent understanding.

Ray had suddenly wanted Patricia and had not resisted, without bothering, I'm sure of it now, about whether his wife would hear of it or not.

"I think the wind is dropping."

Our ears were so used to the din of the storm that we perceived the smallest change in it. That was true. We were still far from silence, but the intensity had gone and looking through the pane we had cleared as well as we could, it seemed that the snowflakes fell almost vertically, though still as thickly.

All over the country teams were working to clear the roads, and ambulances were trying to get through. There were known to be dozens of dead and injured.

"I wonder what is going to happen." It was Mona speaking, as though she were asking herself a question. The snow wouldn't thaw for another two or three weeks. Once the highways were cleared, it would be the turn of our smaller country road. Then teams would come to search for Ray's body.

And after that? They had a lovely apartment in the best and most elegant part of New York, on Sutton Place, on the East River.

Would she go back there to live alone? Would she return to the theater, to television?

She had been right when she spoke a moment ago. It was all unreal, meaningless. As for me, I hadn't thought of Mona's future for a moment, as I had sat meditating on the bench in the barn. Very well, I had killed Ray, I had revenged myself, in a rather mean, cowardly way, without caring about the consequences.

Actually I had killed no one. It was useless to brag about it. I might have gone on blundering in the snow for the rest of the night without a hope in the world of finding my friend.

I had killed him in my mind. In spirit. No, not even that, because that would have demanded a self-control that I hadn't possessed at the time.

"Perhaps we should put some mattresses in front of the fire and try to get some sleep," Isabel suggested. "No, not you, Mona. Let Donald and me do it."

We went to get the mattresses that belong to the two girls—they were light and narrow—and then the one from the spare room. I asked myself, rather stupidly, whether we mightn't put them next to each other, to make one large bed on which we could have slept, all three of us, and I'm certain that Isabel saw what was going through my mind. She left the same space between the mattresses that usually separates twin beds, then she went to get blankets.

It is possible that I might have been wrong. I probably was, but in the short time that we remained alone, Mona and I, she seemed to glance at me, then at the mattresses. Did she ask herself which would be hers and which mine? Did a vague idea cross her mind, rather than a temptation?

When Isabel came back and spread the blankets, we

hesitated for a moment. And this time I'm quite certain of what I say: it wasn't by accident that Isabel chose the mattress to the right, leaving me the middle one and Mona the one on the left. She had purposely put me between them! She was virtually saying:

"You see? I trust you. . . ."

Me or Mona?

True, it could also have meant:

"I give you your freedom. I've always given you your freedom. . . ."

Or even:

"Surely you wouldn't dare . . ."

It was a little after midday and we were all three of us dying to get some sleep. The last thing I remember was Mona's hand on the floor, between our two mattresses, and that hand, as I drifted off to sleep, acquired an incredible meaning. For quite a time, I asked myself whether I dared put out my hand to touch it as if by accident.

I wasn't in love. It was the gesture that mattered, the courage of the gesture. It seemed to me that it would be a deliverance. But my mind must have already been confused, for the image of the hand transformed itself into the image of a dog I recognized, one that had belonged to one of our neighbors when I was twelve.

I must have fallen asleep.

The power came on again a little after ten in the evening, and it was startling to see all the lamps in the house suddenly come on on their own, while the candle went on burning, rather ridiculous now with its little orange flame.

We looked at each other, relieved, as though this were the end of all our troubles and disasters.

I went down to the cellar to switch on the furnace, and when I returned Isabel was trying to telephone.

"Does it work?"

"Not yet. . . ."

I could see in my mind's eye the men outside, climbing the poles with those strange steel horseshoes on their feet that allow them to climb like monkeys. I've always longed to climb like that.

"Where do we sleep?" asked Mona.

"The rooms will take some time to get warm. We'll have to wait two or three hours."

We didn't talk much, that Sunday, neither during the day nor in the evening. If I had taken down all we said, it wouldn't make three pages. Nobody tried to read. Still less was there any desire to play any game. Luckily, the flames were dancing in the fireplace, and we spent most of the time looking at them.

We lay down, dressed, in the same order as in the afternoon, but I didn't see Mona's hand on the floor. Then at a certain moment I heard some noise and saw Isabel standing by the fire, folding a blanket. I didn't have to ask what was going on. She could see the question in my eyes.

"It's six o'clock, the rooms are warm. We had better end the night in our beds."

Mona was still kneeling on her mattress, her face flushed, her eyes full of sleep.

I helped Isabel to carry Mona's mattress to the spare room, and the two women made up the bed. I went to undress in our bedroom, slipped on my pajamas, and was already in bed when my wife came in.

"She is taking it all very calmly," said Isabel.

She herself spoke with great calm, simply stating a nonimportant fact. Later, she touched my shoulder.

"Donald, the telephone . . ."

I thought first that someone was calling us, that the telephone had rung, and my first thought was of Ray. But Isabel had only wanted to say that the telephone was working. The old clock, on the chest of drawers, showed half past seven. I got up to get a glass of water in the bathroom and at the same time combed my hair. Then, sitting on the bed, I called the police station at Canaan.

The line was busy . . . ten, twenty times it was busy, then finally a tired voice . . .

"This is Donald Dodd of Brentwood, Dodd, yes. The lawyer."

"I know you, Mr. Dodd. . . ."

"Whom am I talking to?"

"Sergeant Tomasi. . . . Anything wrong in your part of the world?"

"Is Lieutenant Olsen there?"

"He spent the night here, we all did. Would you like to speak to him?"

"Yes, please, Tomasi. Hello. Lieutenant Olsen?"

"Yes, Olsen speaking."

"This is Dodd."

"Anything wrong?"

Isabel couldn't see my face, as I had my back turned to her, but I was certain that her eyes were fixed on my shoulders, on the nape of my neck, and that she could see me as well as if I were facing her.

"I've got to report a disappearance to you. Last night . . . No, it was the night before . . ."

Time had become confused.

"Saturday night we went to a party at the Ashbridges' with two friends from New York."

"Yes, I know."

Olsen was a tall, fair-haired man with an impassive face, a high complexion, close-cut hair. I had never seen him with a speck of dust on him or a wrong crease on his uniform. I had also never seen him tired or impatient.

"On the way back at night, we got stuck in the snow just this side of the bridge. . . . The battery of our flashlight had practically run out. . . . There were four of us, the two women in front, my friend and I behind, trying to get to the house. . . ."

Silence at the other side of the wire, as if the line had been cut off again. It was embarrassing, and I could still feel Isabel's eyes fixed on my back.

"Are you there?"

"I'm listening, Mr. Dodd."

"The two women reached the house safely. So did I in the end, and it was only then I noticed that my friend wasn't beside me any more."

"Who is he?"

"Ray Sanders, of Miller, Miller and Sanders, the public-relations firm."

"You haven't found him?"

"I went to search for him, without any light to speak of. . . . I blundered about in the snow, and shouted. . . ."

"With that blizzard, he couldn't have heard you unless he had been quite close to you."

"I know. When I came to the end of my strength, I came back. Yesterday morning, yes, yesterday, Sunday, we tried to go out, my wife and I, but the snow was too deep."

"Have you telephoned your nearest neighbors?"

"Not yet. . . . But I presume that if he'd been with any of them, he would have called me up by now."

"It's most probable. . . . Listen. I'm going to send a team out to you. . . . It isn't snowplows we need, it's bulldozers. . . . Only part of the road is more or less free of snow. Call me up if you have any news."

We had, on the whole, done all we could. I was on the right side of the authorities.

"Are they coming?" I heard my wife's steady voice.

"Only a small part of the road is free of snow. He says it's not snowplows they need, but bulldozers. . . . He's trying to send us a team, he doesn't know when. . . ."

She went to the kitchen to make some coffee while I had a shower and put on the same clothes as yesterday, my gray flannel trousers and my old brown pullover.

Isabel had prepared some eggs and bacon for herself and me, and as Mona's place was unoccupied, she said:

"She's asleep."

It seemed to me that, all the same, she was rather surprised at Mona's reactions, or rather at her lack of reactions. Would she have behaved differently if I'd been the one that had been lost in the blizzard?

I realized suddenly the sort of void that I had become aware of since my wife had waked me up by touching my shoulder: the wind had stopped blowing. The world outside had become silent; it was a silence that seemed unnatural after the hours of din we had gone through.

I switched on the television set. I saw roofs torn off, cars buried in the snow, fallen trees, a bus lying upside down in a street in Hartford. I also saw streets in New York being hastily cleared and a few solitary figures trying to make their way on the sidewalks.

There had been no sign of life from several ships at sea. One house had been carried away by the wind. Another had toppled onto its side, supported by a mountain of snow.

There were four or more feet of snow at our own door, and we could do nothing but wait. . . .

I called up three neighbors, Lancaster, the electrician, whose house is half a mile away from us as the crow flies, Glendale, the C.P.A., and finally an individual I don't care for, a certain Cameron, vaguely concerned with real estate.

"It's Donald Dodd speaking. Forgive me for disturbing you. . . . Has a friend of mine, by any chance, taken shelter with you?"

None of the three had seen him. Cameron was the only one to ask what he looked like before he answered.

"He's tall, about forty, brown hair."

"His name?"

"Ray Sanders. . . . Have you seen him?"

"No. I've seen no one."

When I went back to the kitchen Mona was eating there. Unlike Isabel, she hadn't dressed properly and her hair was falling over her face. She smelled of bed. Isabel never smells of bed; as my mother used to say, she smells clean.

This disarray of Mona's, her almost animal self-neglect, disturbed me, and the dumb, questioning look in her eyes, as she half whispered to me: "When will they be coming?" distressed me too.

"As soon as they can. They are on their way now, but they have to wait for the snow to be cleared away a bit."

Isabel was looking from one to the other of us, but I had no idea what she was thinking. If she herself could read other people's thoughts, nobody could read hers.

In spite of that, she had the most open face imaginable. She inspired confidence in everyone. Whatever she got engaged in, she always found herself saddled with the trickiest and often most unpleasant details, and she dealt with them with the same serene expression.

"Isabel is always there when she's needed."

To comfort, to advise, to help . . . Apart from a daily helper, who came for three hours a day and one full day a week, she looked after the house and did the cooking. It was she who looked after our girls, and attended to their education, before they went to the Adams boarding school, because there was no suitable school for them at Brentwood.

There was perhaps a little snobbery in that. Isabel had been to the Adams school in Litchfield herself, and it was considered the most select in Connecticut. Yet Isabel was no snob. I had lived seventeen years with her. For seventeen years we had slept in the same room. We had, I suppose, made love several thousands of times. But up to this moment I have no complete picture of her in my mind.

I know her features, the color of her skin, the blond sheen of her hair that is tinged with red, the broad shoulders that are growing a little heavy, the calm gestures, her walk. She dresses mostly in pale blue, but her favorite color is deep lilac. I know her smile, never very pronounced, a slightly cautious smile, which nevertheless warms the natural serenity of her face.

But what, for example, does she think about, the whole day long? What does she think of me, her husband and the father of her daughters? What are her real feelings where I'm concerned?

What does she think at this very moment of Mona, who is finishing her eggs?

She cannot be fond of Mona, who represents a certain carelessness, even disorder, and God knows what else, and who is so much her opposite. Mona's past is not as simple and straightforward as her own. In Mona's past there are Broadway nights, the backstage of theaters, the actors' and actresses' dressing rooms, and her father, who wasn't embarrassed to leave his daughter in the care of one or another of his mistresses.

Mona hadn't cried. She wasn't even miserable. She rather gave one the impression of someone who finds things beginning to drag.

Her husband was somewhere in the snow, maybe three or four hundred feet away from the house, a house that was not hers, where she couldn't get on with her usual routine and must feel a prisoner. Now that the storm was over and the snow had stopped, the light had come back and one could communicate by telephone and see the world live again on the television screen, one still had to wait for a team to come from Canaan and begin to move thousands of cubic feet of snow.

"I've run out of cigarettes," she announced, pushing away her plate.

I went to get her a package from the liquor cupboard. It suddenly struck me that we had been eating in the kitchen, whereas normally, when we had guests, we ate in the dining room, even breakfast. Even when we were alone, Isabel and I, we had lunch and dinner in the dining room. We had taken the mattresses to the rooms on the top floor, and the dirty glasses had disappeared.

"I'll give you a hand. . . ."

Mona was wearing her black slacks, her canary-yellow sweater. She helped my wife to do the dishes, and I didn't know what to do with myself. I had too much time to think. I asked myself too many questions that embarrassed me.

All these questions didn't just date from the time I

had spent on the bench in the barn. I hadn't lived seventeen years without bringing them up.

How was it that up to now they had never disturbed me? Probably I had answered them automatically, but adequately, in the way you are taught to answer questions at school. Father. Mother. Children. Love. Marriage. Fidelity. Kindness. Devotion . . .

It's true that I had lived like that. Even as a citizen I accepted my duties with the same earnestness as Isabel. Was it possible that I never realized that I was lying to myself and that in fact I didn't believe in these impeccable images?

In our office, it is my colleague, Higgins, whom I always call old Higgins, though he is only sixty, who deals with sales and acquisitions of property, mortgages, incorporations, and generally with the technical side of the business.

He is a chubby, foxy individual who, in a different age, might have been seen at the fairground selling the elixir of youth. He is rather dirty and unkempt, and I suspect him of exaggerating the vulgarity of his manner the better to cheat his fellow beings.

He believes in nothing and in no one and often shocks me by his cynicism.

As for me, my domain is more personal, for it concerns wills, probates, and divorces. I have settled hundreds of them, for our clientele stretches way beyond Brentwood and many rich people live in the district.

I'm not talking of crime. I don't think I've pleaded more than ten cases in a court of law.

I should have had some knowledge of human beings. Both men and women. I thought I knew them, and yet in my private life I behaved and formed my judgments according to what one might call the good books.

I have remained, in fact, a boy scout.

Yet on the bench . . .

I don't know where the two women are, probably in the spare room, and I drag about, alone, in the living room and in the library, ruminating over thoughts of which I'm not proud.

I who had imagined I thought clearly. It had been enough just to witness a man and a woman making love in a bathroom. For that, certainly, was the starting point. Anyway, the apparent starting point. There must have been other motives, other images, further back, that I shall discover only later.

It was on the red bench, in the barn with the banging door, that a truth was revealed to me that changed everything.

"I hate him. . . ."

I hate him and I will let him die. I hate him and I will kill him. I hate him because he's stronger than I am, because he has a more desirable wife than I have, because he leads the life I would have liked to lead, because he goes ahead with no thought for those he pushes aside on his way.

I'm not a weak man. Neither am I a failure. It is I who have chosen my life, in the same way as I chose Isabel.

The idea of marrying Mona, for instance, would

have never occurred to me, had I met her at that time. Nor would I have thought of joining a public-relations firm. That choice was not made from a lack of temerity nor out of laziness. The pattern becomes much more complicated. I'm approaching a territory where I fear I may make some painful discoveries.

Take the case of Isabel. I met her at a dance, actually in Litchfield, where she lived with her parents. Her father was Irving Whitaker, the surgeon, who was constantly summoned to Boston and farther afield. As for her mother, she was a Clayburn, old American stock. It wasn't her father's reputation or her mother's name that had influenced me. Neither was it Isabel's beauty nor her physical attraction.

I had been sexually stirred by other girls much more than I had by her.

Was it her calm? The kind of serenity which she already had in those days? Her gentleness? Her tolerance?

But why should I have been looking for tolerance, when I was doing no wrong?

The truth is that I wanted to have everything run smoothly and orderly around me.

And now I have a desperate desire for a woman like Mona, who is the exact opposite!

The important thing, my father used to say, is to choose well at the start.

He didn't mean only the choice of a woman, but of a profession, of a way of life, a way of thinking. . . .

I believed I had chosen. I had done the best I could, and I had made a supreme effort to do it. Little by little

I reached the point when all I wanted was Isabel's approval.

What I had chosen was a witness, a favorable witness, someone who would testify to me that I was on the right road.

All this was destroyed in a single night. What I envied in Ray, as I envied it in a man like Ashbridge, was that they were self-sufficient, that they did not need the approval of anyone.

Ashbridge didn't care that people laughed behind his back because his three successive wives were anything but faithful to him. He chose them beautiful, young, sensual, and he knew beforehand what he had to expect from them.

Did it really matter?

And Ray—did he really love Mona? Was it a matter of complete indifference to him that she had slept with a lot of men before him? Was it they who were the strong men and I the weak one because I had chosen to be at peace with myself?

Well, I hadn't found it, that peace. I had only pretended to have found it. I had spent seventeen years of my life pretending.

I could hear a droning sound outside, and when I opened the door it increased. I realized that the snowplows were arriving, and I thought I could pick out men's voices.

Would they find Ray today? It wasn't likely. Mona would spend at least another night in the house, and I regretted that it wouldn't, like the first night, be on a mattress in the living room. I suddenly remembered her hand on the floor, the hand that I had had such a violent desire to touch, as if it were a symbol.

I was trying to escape. But to escape from what?

For more than twenty-four hours I had known that actually I was a cruel man, capable of rejoicing over a man's death, a man, moreover, whom I had considered my best friend, and capable, if necessary, of provoking that death.

"You're freezing us to death. . . ."

I quickly shut the door and saw the two women, who had been dressing. Mona was wearing a red dress, my wife a pale blue one. It seemed as if they were trying desperately to return to everyday life.

This didn't make it any the less false.

III

Toward four o'clock, through the window we saw the plows slowly attacking the snow, cutting great trenches through it, piling up walls of it as steep as cliffs. It was fascinating. We didn't say a word. We just watched—our minds blank. At least, as far as I was concerned, my mind was a blank. Since Saturday night I had been outside my normal life, in a way beyond life altogether.

What I remember best is my awareness of a female in the house. You could say that I was sniffing her like a dog, that I searched for her as soon as she disappeared from my view, that I padded around her waiting for an opportunity to touch her.

I had a crazy, irrational, voluptuous desire to touch her. Did Mona know? She never mentioned Ray, except perhaps two or three times. I wondered if she, too, was desperate for a releasing, physical contact. And there was Isabel's look that followed us, without any anxiety, with perhaps just a slight astonishment. She was so accustomed to the man I had been for so many years that she had hardly any need to look at me.

Still, she must have noticed the change. She could not

have helped but notice it. And she could not yet fathom at once what it meant.

I could see a huge snowplow emerging several yards away from the house, forging ahead as though it were going to continue its course straight through the living room. The monster stopped in time. I opened the door.

"Come in and have a drink."

There were three of them. And two more in a car behind. They came in, all five men, in their lumber jackets, their huge boots, and one of them had hoarfrost on his mustache. Their presence alone brought a chill into the room.

Isabel had gone to get glasses and whisky. They looked around, surprised by the calm, intimate atmosphere of the house. Then they looked at Mona. Not at Isabel, at Mona. Did they, too, emerging from their silent battle with the snow, respond to the sensuality of the woman?

"Your good health. And thanks for rescuing us."

"The lieutenant is on his way. He has been told the road's free now."

They were the kind of people that one sees only on rare occasions, like chimney sweeps, and who, the rest of the time, live God knows where. There was only one whose face seemed familiar, and I couldn't recall where I had seen him before.

"Thank you, Mister. It sure warms you up."

"Another drink?"

"We'd like to, but we've got to push on."

The ungainly monsters departed, covered with white

powder, and soon after, in the growing darkness, we saw at the end of the trench the pale headlights of a car.

Two men in uniform got out of it, Lieutenant Olsen and another man whose name I didn't know. It was I who opened the door to them while the two women remained sitting in their chairs.

"Good evening, Lieutenant. I'm sorry to have to get you out . . ."

"You have no news of your friend?"

He went to greet Isabel, whom he had met before, and I introduced him to Mona.

"This is my friend Ray Sanders' wife. . . ."

He sat in the chair offered to him. His companion, a young man, did the same.

"You don't mind if I ask you a few questions, Mrs. Sanders?"

He pulled a notebook and a pen out of his pocket.

"You say Ray Sanders. What address?"

"We live on Sutton Place, Manhattan."

"What is your husband's profession?"

"He's partner in a public-relations firm, Miller, Miller and Sanders. . . ."

"And before?"

"First he was legal adviser to the Millers and their associate for three years."

"Legal adviser . . ." Olsen repeated, as if to himself.

I intervened:

"We studied together at Yale, Ray and I. . . . He was my oldest friend."

There was neither rhyme nor reason for my saying that.

"You were on your way somewhere else?" he asked Mona.

It was I who replied:

"Ray and his wife came to see us on their way from Canada. They were to spend the weekend with us."

"Did you come here often?"

The question puzzled me, for I didn't see the point of it. Mona replied this time:

"Two or three times a year."

He glanced at her searchingly, as though her physical appearance was important.

"When did you arrive, you and your husband?"

"On Saturday, about two o'clock."

"Did you have any trouble with the snow on the way?"

"Not much. We were driving slowly. . . ."

"You told me, Mr. Dodd, that you took your friends to the Ashbridges'?"

"That's correct."

"Did they know each other?"

"No. As you probably know, when old Ashbridge gives a party, he doesn't mind whom you take along. . . ."

The lieutenant smiled faintly, as though he knew quite a lot about old Ashbridge's parties.

"Did your husband have a lot to drink?" he asked Mona.

"I wasn't with him most of the time. Yes, I think he must have drunk quite a bit."

It seemed to me that Olsen had quite a lot of information on hand already, probably by telephoning around before he came.

"And you, Mr. Dodd?"

"Yes. I had had a lot to drink."

Isabel was looking at me, her hands folded in her lap.

"More than usual?"

"Yes, I have to admit, much more than usual."

"Were you drunk?"

"Not really, but I wasn't in my normal condition."

Why did I feel forced to add:

"It's only happened a couple of times in my whole life."

Was it a need to be frank? Or was it defiance?

"A couple of times!" exclaimed Olsen. "That's not very much!"

"No."

"Was there any reason why you drank so much?"

"No. I began with two or three whiskies, to get myself in the right mood, then I started to empty all the glasses that came my way. . . . You know how it is. . . ."

I was being very much myself, very much the lawyer, speaking with precision.

"Did your friend Ray drink with you?"

"We bumped into each other several times, had a few words together when we found ourselves in the same group, then we were separated again. . . . It's a very big house, you know, and there were people everywhere."

"And you, Mrs. Sanders?"

She glanced at me, as though seeking advice, then turned to Isabel.

"Yes, I drank, too," she admitted.

"A lot?"

"I guess so. . . . I stayed for some time with Isabel. . . ."

"And with your husband?"

"I only saw him from a distance, two or three times. . . ."

"Who was he with?"

"With various people I don't know. He had a long talk with Mr. Ashbridge, I remember that; they both stood in a corner, discussing something. . . ."

"On the whole, your husband behaved as usual on these occasions?"

"Yes. . . . Why do you ask?"

She looked at me again, surprised.

"I'm obliged to put these questions to you; it's routine in cases of disappearance. . . ."

"But this is an accident!"

"I don't doubt it, Mrs. Sanders. . . . Your husband had no reason to commit suicide, had he?"

"None."

She opened her eyes very wide.

"Nor to disappear, leaving no trace?"

"Why should he want to disappear?"

"Do you have children?"

"No."

"How long have you been married?"

"Twelve years."

"Did your husband meet anyone he had known before at the Ashbridges'?"

I began to feel uneasy.

"Not that I know of."

"A woman?"

"I saw him talking to many women. He is always very popular."

"There was no quarrel? No incident that comes to your mind?"

A flush rose to Mona's face, and I knew she was aware of what had happened between Ray and Patricia. Had she opened the bathroom door, as I had done? Had she seen them come out of the bedroom?

"You were among the last to leave?"

Now it was obvious that the lieutenant already had all the details.

"When we went, there were only about half a dozen people left, I suppose."

"Who was driving?"

"I was."

"You were lucky, you know, when you think of the weather. . . . Another good push and you would have been home. . . ."

"Yes, I know. . . ."

I had been listening to a new noise outside in the last few minutes. Turning to the window, I saw a steam shovel working under an arc light in the now total darkness.

Olsen answered my unspoken question.

"I ordered the search to begin in spite of the darkness, just in case. One never knows. . . ."

One never knows what? Whether Ray was still alive?

"When you left the car, you walked on in the dark."

"The flashlight was hardly working. I thought it was better for the two women to go in front."

"That was right."

Isabel, motionless in her chair, was observing us one after the other; she followed the answers on our lips as if she were gathering up all the threads of the story, knitting with her eyes. Perhaps the threads would all be knit together one day.

"We kept very close to each other," she said.

"Were the men far away from you?"

"No, quite close. . . . The noise of the wind was so strong we could hardly hear when they called out to us."

"You had no difficulty in finding the house?"

"Actually, I wasn't too sure where I was. . . . I think I came here just by instinct."

"Looking back, you couldn't see the light?"

"A little, at the beginning. . . . It soon faded out, though, and then it disappeared altogether."

"How long after you did your husband get there?"

She looked at me as though asking my advice. She wasn't confused. Nor did she appear to find these questions peculiar, in the circumstances.

"A minute, perhaps. I wanted to switch on the light and realized the current was off. I asked Mona if she had any matches. I went to the dining room to light a candle, and then Donald came in. . . ."

What could the lieutenant be writing in his notebook, and what use would these notes be to him? Then he turned to me again.

"Did you have any trouble finding the house?"

"I literally bumped into it when I thought I had still some way to go. I was beginning to wonder if I'd lost my bearings."

"And your friend?"

"I presumed he was beside me. . . . I mean within a few feet of me. . . . Every now and again I called out to him."

"Did he reply?"

"I thought I heard him several times but the din was so terrible . . ."

"And then?"

"When I saw that Ray wasn't there . . ."

"How long did you wait?"

"About five minutes."

"Did you have another flashlight at home?"

"Yes, in our room. We hardly ever used it, so we hadn't checked on the refills and they were no good either."

"You went off alone?"

"My wife and Mona were exhausted."

"And what about you?"

"I was, too."

"How did you make your way?"

"As best I could. My idea was to keep going round and round and make wider and wider circles. . . ."

"You weren't afraid you'd slip over the steep rocks?"

"I thought I could avoid it. When you have lived in a place for fifteen years . . . Several times I had to get down on my knees."

"Did you go to your car?"

I looked at the two women. I had forgotten what I had said to them about the car. I went a bit blank for a second, then I staked everything on one card.

"I reached it by accident."

"It was empty, of course."

"Yes. I rested for a bit, and sheltered by it."

"And the barn? Did you make sure he was not in the barn?"

I was suddenly scared, for the first time during this unexpected interrogation. It seemed to me that Olsen knew something, something that I didn't even know myself, and that he was setting traps for me, in all innocence, of course, as he went on scribbling in his notebook.

"I found that because of the noise of the door that's off its hinges. . . . I shouted Ray's name but I heard nothing in reply."

"You went in?"

"Yes, I guess I did step in. . . ."

"I see."

He closed his notebook and got up, very much the officer.

"I must thank all three of you; I'm sorry for disturbing you like this. . . . The search will go on all night if the weather conditions permit."

Then, turning to Mona:

"I suppose you will stay here, Mrs. Sanders?"

"Why . . . of course."

Where else could she go while they searched for her husband's body in mountains of snow?

We had dinner. I remember that Isabel warmed up some canned spaghetti and meat balls. What day was it? Monday. I did nothing the whole day. I didn't go to the office; it would have been impossible, but nevertheless I felt guilty about it.

In the morning it was usually I who went to get the mail in the mailbox. My days kept a very definite pattern, to which I had been attached. There was a precise time for every single thing, almost for my every action.

I was all the time conscious of Mona's presence and wondered if something would happen. Not here, presumably. But why not? She had just lost her husband, whose body was being searched for by those strong men and their great machines outside.

"Ray was a good sort. . . ."

For the last three days we had, all three of us, been living on our nerves, she in particular. Mightn't that just be the moment to turn for comfort elsewhere?

Men at war purge their fears through sexual release.

If we were alone in a room for a while and could be sure Isabel wouldn't come in . . .

Nothing had happened so far. We went to look at the shovel through the window, and I barely managed to touch Mona's elbow.

We went to bed. Mona alone, Isabel and I in our room.

"What do you think of Olsen?"

The question surprised me, for it indicated my wife's line of thought. And I, myself, had been thinking of Olsen.

"He's decent enough. He has the reputation of knowing his business."

I was expecting the conversation to go on, but Isabel went no further and gave no indication of what else was going through her mind.

Only later, when we were ready to turn out the lights, she murmured:

"I don't believe Mona is really suffering."

I replied evasively:

"You can never tell. . . ."

"They seemed so attached to one another. . . ."

The word astonished me. "Attached." It is, of course, a current expression, but I suppose that people who use it have forgotten its meaning. Two people "attached to one another . . ."

Why not chained together?

"Good night, Isabel."

"Good night, Donald."

She gave a sigh, as she did every night, to mark the end of her day and the passage to a night's rest. Almost at once she was asleep, while I lay for more than an hour trying to get some sleep.

Mona was alone in the spare room. What was she thinking about? What position was she lying in? I could hear the noise of the shovel outside and visualized the men who were literally sifting the snow.

I woke up with a start in the middle of the night and, not hearing any more noise, wondered if they had found Ray. Why, in that case, didn't they come and tell us?

I didn't move. I asked myself if, in her sleep, Isabel hadn't become conscious of the fact that I was awake and was also listening. She didn't move either, but her breathing became quieter. Everything was silent except an engine, far away, near the post office.

I was unaccountably anxious. This sudden peace seemed menacing to me, and it was with relief that I heard an engine begin abruptly to operate again.

Had something broken down? Had they repaired or oiled it? Or had the men simply needed a drink?

I fell asleep again, and when I woke up it was morning. The smell of coffee already filled the house, soon it would be the smell of bacon and eggs. I got up, slipped on my bathrobe, brushed my teeth, combed my hair, and in my slippers went to the kitchen, which was empty. There was no one in the dining room or living room, either. I presumed that Isabel was with Mona. The engine was still working; it had now turned around the rock and was just underneath it.

A silhouette appeared near the barn and I was astonished to recognize my wife. She had put on my lumber jacket and her boots and moved as best she could in the mass of snow.

Had she seen me behind the window? The living room was in darkness, for I hadn't turned on the light. I don't know why I chose not to be there when she returned. That visit to the barn had something clandestine about it and obviously concerned the lieutenant's questions and my replies.

I drew back from the window, went to our room, and began to fill the tub.

I half hoped that Isabel would come and join me. I had an urgent need for contact with her, to see if anything had changed in the expression of her eyes.

She had heard the water running, and certainly she must have heard that Mona was up and about, for when I went into the kitchen eggs and bacon were cooking for the three of us and the table was set in the dining room.

"Good morning, Mona."

Today she was wearing a very close-fitting black dress, and perhaps because her face showed signs of fatigue, she had put on more make-up than usual, particularly around the eyes, and she looked different.

"Good morning, Donald."

I kissed my wife's cheek.

"Good morning, Isabel."

She didn't return my kiss. It was traditional. I don't know how and when the tradition had been established. It reminded me of my mother, who never kissed me and automatically gave me her cheek or her forehead to kiss.

I realized at once that Isabel knew everything. I had known what my mistake was the day before, when Lieutenant Olsen was questioning us. All the time I had been in the barn, on the red bench, I had chain-smoked, lighting one cigarette after another, dropping the butts on the ground and stamping them out with my foot. I had smoked at least ten.

That was what Isabel had gone to look for, while I was asleep: the proof of my long wait in the barn when I was supposed to be searching for Ray.

She knew. Yet there was no accusation in her blue eyes, no sharpened attitude. Only a slight astonishment and curiosity.

She wasn't looking at me as at a stranger, because of what I had done—I had become someone else, someone she had known for a long time, without understanding his true personality.

We were eating, as we listened to the men working at the foot of the rock. Mona, intrigued by the silence, glanced at us in turn and maybe was asking herself if my wife was jealous.

I gathered this when she said:

"I feel guilty for imposing on you so long."

"You're crazy, Mona. You know perfectly well we've always thought of you and Ray as part of the family. . . ."

I ate quickly, ill at ease. When I got up I said:

"I'll go and see if I can get the car in. . . ."

I put on my boots, my windbreaker, my fur hat. I had a feeling that Mona wanted to suggest accompanying me to get some air but that she didn't dare.

The men below were working more cautiously now, for they had reached the place where there was the best chance of finding the body.

I followed the trench, which was slippery now because of the frozen ground, and found some relief in being outside, in the fresh air, in a world that was familiar in spite of the obvious change in it.

They had pushed my car against the solid wall of snow. It was still under its white blanket and I had to clear the windshield. I wondered if I was going to be able to start the engine again. It occurred to me that after such a long time it was bound to be damaged. But the Chrysler purred again immediately, and I drove it carefully to the front of the garage. It was a little wooden building painted white that stood exactly opposite the barn. I had to clear away some snow with a spade in order to open the door, and inside I saw the Lincoln in which Ray and Mona had arrived from Canada on Saturday afternoon.

A few minutes later I went into the barn. The door had dropped off altogether. There was a carpeting of snow, but it didn't reach the bench. I looked at the ground. The cigarette butts had disappeared.

When I went back into the house I searched her eyes, and she didn't turn her head away. Her eyes looked back at me quite calmly. What could I read in them?

"Yes! I know! I suspected it. When you answered Olsen's question about the barn; I understood then. I went to see and did what I did so the others wouldn't know."

That they shouldn't know that I had been a coward? Did she think that it was physical cowardice, a fear of losing myself in the blizzard that had prompted me to take shelter in the barn?

If that weren't so why was there no contempt in her expression? Nor any pity. There was no anger. Nothing. Yes, there was something! There was curiosity.

Almost in a whisper, she said:

"Did you have trouble with the car?"

"No."

"Are you going to the office?"

"I'm going to telephone Helen and ask her to bring the mail. I don't think there'll be any: I don't expect they have been able to get around with it."

We were talking in a vacuum. She had seen me go into the barn. Obviously I must have discovered that she had dealt with the cigarette butts.

The dishwashing had already been done. We looked at each other, the three of us, not knowing where to go or what to do. Mona must have become more aware every minute that there was something in the air, and she turned away in embarrassment.

"I'll go and tidy my room."

The cleaning woman hadn't arrived. She lived on the other side of the hill, and the road from the village, through the woods, probably had not been cleared yet.

"On second thought, I think I'll go to the office."

It was intolerable to be caught like that, waiting for the men to discover the body. I brought out the car which I had just driven into the garage. Once I was off our land, I found the road less snowbound, with tire marks of the cars that had already got through. The highway appeared to be almost normal apart from the two walls of snow on either side of the road.

Most of the storekeepers were out with spades, digging paths to their shops. The post office was open, and I went in, greeting the man at the counter as I usually did, as though nothing untoward had happened. There were only a few letters in our mailbox and a handful of circulars. Then I went to the office.

Nothing had changed there, either. Higgins was in his room and looked up at me with some surprise.

"So they've found him, after all?"

I frowned.

"I mean your friend, Sanders—are they still searching in the snow?"

Five years ago, on the site of the old offices, we had built a pretty house of pink brick, with the windows framed in white. The door, too, was white. Around it was a well-kept lawn which of course could not be seen at the moment, but which re-emerged every year with the sun in the middle of March, or toward the end.

Helen, our secretary, was typing in her room and didn't interrupt her work to greet me.

Everything was calm and in perfect order, my lawbooks on their mahogany shelves. The hands of the electric clock moved noiselessly.

I sat down in my armchair and opened the letters one after the other.

"Helen!"

"Yes, Mr. Dodd?"

She was twenty-five and rather attractive. The daughter of one of our clients, a builder, she had married six months ago. Would she stay with us if she had a child?

She had said she would, but I wasn't so sure and could see that in time we would have to replace her.

I dictated three unimportant letters.

"The others are for Higgins."

Had it been a shock to Isabel? Was our life going to be affected by it? I was asking myself that question, without really knowing whether I wanted to know the answer or not. The exalted mood of that night in the barn had dissipated, but something of it still remained, nevertheless.

My wife was right to look at me questioningly. I was not the same man. Higgins had not noticed it, neither had my secretary. But sooner or later they would notice the transformation.

I looked at my watch as though I had an appointment to keep. And in fact I did have one. Only it hadn't any fixed time. I longed for the search around Yellow Rock Farm to be over, for Ray's body to be discovered. I wanted to be finished with it all. What would happen after that? It didn't concern me. It was Mona's business. And she was busy making her bed, tidying her room. There were no newspapers. The New York train hadn't arrived. Helen brought me my three letters to sign much sooner than I had expected.

"I'm going home. . . . If you need me for anything, you can telephone."

I went to Higgins' room, shook hands with him, and left.

Once outside, it occurred to me to buy some meat, and I went to the supermarket.

"Have they found your friend, Mr. Dodd?"

"Not yet. . . ."

"When you think that things like that can happen right here among us, without our even knowing it! . . . Is there much damage at your place?"

"No, only the door of the barn."

"One of the houses in Cresthill collapsed. It was a miracle no one was killed."

Our cleaning woman lived at Cresthill. . . .

All the time I was talking and looking around making all the routine gestures I was asking myself:

"What is she thinking now?"

If I knew her, she wouldn't mention it at all. Our life would go on as usual with this secret between us. From time to time I would feel her eyes on me and doubtless they would continue to express the same degree of surprise.

As I took the left turn up the lane leading to our house I noticed that the engines were no longer in action, and a few minutes later I saw the two women in the distance emerging from the house in their boots and parkas. At the foot of the rock the men gathered around a figure on the ground.

Ray had been found. I took the car to the garage. I was calm, I had no feeling of guilt. On the contrary, only an immense relief. The women were waiting for me. I gave each of them a hand, but it didn't prevent us from slipping on the rocks, and the men had to help us up.

Ray looked as if he were smiling under the soft layer of snow which still covered his face and made his hair look prematurely white. His right leg was twisted and one of the men told us that it was broken.

I wondered what Mona was going to do. She didn't hurry to the body. Perhaps she did want to, for a moment, because she took two or three steps in that direction. Then she stopped and shuddered. My wife was on her right side, I was on her left.

It was to me she turned, only slightly, just enough to touch my shoulder and my side, as though she needed the protective warmth of my body. Then, with a glance at Isabel, I put my arm around her shoulders.

"Be brave, Mona. . . ."

It was a natural gesture. She was the wife of my best friend. The men standing around us must have found it perfectly natural. Nor did Mona find it strange; she seemed to want to come even closer. It was only I who, for some reason, found it necessary to throw a defiant glance at Isabel. It represented another milestone, as if, by this gesture, simple as it was, I was pointing out to her that I was free.

She didn't waver, she turned again to look at the body, her hands folded in prayer, as one does in a cemetery, watching the coffin being lowered into the ground.

"Do you want us to carry him into the house?"

The foreman came up.

"The lieutenant asked that nothing should be done before he gets here."

"You called him?"

"Yes, I was instructed to do that."

We couldn't stay there, in the cold, our feet buried in the snow, waiting for the lieutenant to come from Canaan.

"Let's go in, Mona. . . ."

I thought she would protest, but she allowed herself to be led away and we had to climb back up the slope, helping one another. I no longer had my arm around her shoulders, but I had held it there. It was a victory.

"I suppose he slipped," she said when we got to the top. "Poor Ray. . . ."

We were walking, the three of us, three somber silhouettes in a white landscape; it must have been grotesque. The men, below us, were turning on their engines again and most probably were going to work elsewhere.

"Will you make some coffee, Isabel?"

We followed her to the kitchen, where she was putting the kettle on to boil. It was she who put the question:

"What are you going to do, Mona?"

"I don't know."

"Has he got a family?"

"A brother who is in the Embassy in Germany."

"He never said anything to you?"

"What about?"

"About what to do if anything . . ." Calm, she was searching for words and found them.

"If anything happened to him. . . ."

"He never spoke of that. . . ."

"It's what we have to think of now," continued Isabel, undertaking as usual the most painful duty. "Do you think he left a will?"

Mona said "No," and at the same time I broke in.

"If he had made a will, he would have left it with me . . . made it with me. . . ."

"Do you think that he would have wanted to be cremated, Mona?"

"I don't know."

Each of us took his cup of coffee into the living room, and looking outside we saw the police car arrive; the lieutenant and another man in uniform got out of it by the rock.

About ten minutes later the lieutenant came in alone, taking off his cap.

"My condolences, Mrs. Sanders."

"Thank you. . . ."

"It was as you thought, Mr. Dodd. He lost his way near the rock and slipped, and broke his leg in the fall."

Had I said that to him? It struck me that he, too, was looking at me rather peculiarly.

"I'm going to have the body taken to the mortuary and all you'll have to do then is to give the necessary instructions."

"Yes," murmured Mona without seeming to know what was expected of her.

"Where will you bury him?"

"I don't know. . . ."

I suggested:

"At Pleasantville?"

It's a big cemetery in New York.

"Yes, of course. . . ."

"Has he any family?"

"A brother, in Germany."

It all began again. Words. Lips that moved. But I did not listen to the words. I looked at the eyes. I think that I have always looked at the eyes. I think I have always been a little afraid of them. . . .

There were Isabel's. I knew those. Ever since the morning I had been aware of the astonishment in them. Yet it was she who was carefully watching the lieutenant. She had noticed how he kept glancing at me from time to time, as if something in the story was bothering him.

I'm certain that if the lieutenant had attacked me she would have leaped to my defense. Perhaps she was only waiting for that very moment.

As for Mona, it was to me she turned every time they asked her a question, as if I had become her natural support. It was so obvious, there was such confidence, such an abandon in her attitude, that Olsen was bound to have thought there was some intimate bond between us.

Was that why he was less than cordial toward me? I found him almost contemptuous.

"I leave you to do what is necessary. Our job is finished now. I'm sorry, Mrs. Sanders, that this tragedy had to happen here."

He rose, bowed to the two women, and finally shook my hand. Was it sincere? I'm not so sure. There was something mysterious in the air. Either the men had discovered something irregular that put me in a delicate position or else Olsen believed me to be the lover of my best friend's wife and despised me for it.

Did he imagine I had taken the opportunity of getting rid of Ray by pushing him over the rock?

I hadn't thought of that before. It was so plausible, so simple! And why, in fact, had I made the women walk in front, when I was the only one who had a flashlight, inadequate as it was?

The rock is more familiar to me than to anyone else, as it is on my land, right in front of my windows. I could have taken Ray's arm, taken him off course, toward the right, and then pushed him. . . .

I was terrified to think that Olsen might have found the cigarette butts by the bench in the barn. Would he have drawn the same conclusions as Isabel? What were, in fact, Isabel's conclusions? What was there to prove that she did not think I had given Ray a push?

In that case her silence was a sort of complicity. A defense of our home, of our two children?

Her eyes followed me when I opened the liquor cupboard.

"A drink would do you good, Mona. What about you, Isabel?"

"No, thank you. . . ."

I went to get some ice and glasses in the kitchen. Handing Mona her drink, I said:

"Courage, Mona darling."

As though I were taking possession of her. This time

she noticed it and for a moment looked surprised. I had never called her "darling."

"I'm going to telephone the undertaker," said Isabel, going to the library, where there was an extension. Was it so that she could leave us alone?

After a sip of her drink, Mona turned to me with a sad smile.

"You are sweet, Donald. . . ."

Then, glancing in Isabel's direction, she seemed to want to say something more, but finally decided to keep silent.

IV

The funeral took place on Thursday morning and was quite unlike anything I had imagined it was going to be, when the three of us were isolated in our house. Disasters and illnesses must have much in common. It seems impossible that things will ever be normal again, that life will ever be the same, and then one realizes that the daily routine has in fact taken over quite quickly.

There were more than twenty cars at ten o'clock in front of Fred Dowling's funeral chapel, about a hundred feet from my office, and two of them had brought journalists and photographers from New York.

Some had come the day before to the house. They had insisted on photographing Mona on the spot where Ray's body had been found.

Bob Sanders had arrived the day before from Bonn. Isabel had suggested that he spend the night in one of the girls' rooms, but he had already reserved a room at the Turley Hotel.

He was taller, thinner, more unconcerned than Ray. He was even more easy in his manner than his elder brother had been, and I didn't care for his self-confident smile. I had met him several times when we were students, but he was much younger than we were and I hadn't paid much attention to him.

He didn't seem too friendly with Mona.

"How did it happen? Was he drunk?"

"No, he hadn't drunk more than usual."

"Was he drinking a lot, then?"

Ray had been five years his senior, but the way he spoke made him sound like a judge pronouncing sentence.

"No . . . two or three Martinis before meals."

He had been born near New Haven and knew our climate. He must have seen plenty of blizzards, perhaps not on the same scale as the one on Saturday, but fairly devastating all the same.

"How was it he wasn't discovered earlier?"

"In some places there were more than four feet of snow."

"What steps did you take?"

He wasn't particularly fond of me, either. He glanced at me now and then frowning, thinking, perhaps, that I had been in too great a hurry to take Mona under my protection.

For I was doing it on purpose, quite blatantly. I stood beside her. It was I who answered most of the questions, and I felt that this exasperated him.

"Whom have you informed of his death?"

"His associates, of course. . . ."

"Did you give the news to the papers?"

"No. . . . It must have been someone from the village. . . . One of the policemen, perhaps. . . . A whisky?"

"No, thank you. I don't drink."

He had hired a drive-yourself car at the airport. He was married. His wife and his three children lived with him in Bonn. He had come alone. I think he hadn't seen Ray for several years.

The Miller brothers, on the other hand, didn't trouble themselves to come to the house. It was only in the funeral parlor that they came up to Mona to offer their condolences. I knew one of them, Samuel—we had once lunched with him and Ray in New York. He was a man of about sixty, bald and jovial.

He came up to me and asked in an undertone:

"Do you know who is taking care of the will?"

"It's up to Mona."

"Has she talked to you about it?"

"Not yet."

He went to talk to the brother about it and asked the same question, for I saw Bob shake his head.

Mona was driving her own car, for from Pleasantville she was going direct to New York. I suggested that Isabel should do the driving, but Mona refused, though she let Isabel sit beside her.

Following the two women came the brother's car, then mine, then the chauffeur-driven limousine of the Miller brothers, who looked like twins.

Other people from Madison Avenue followed, including Ray's secretary, a Junoesque red-haired girl who seemed much more upset than Mona.

There were many faces I didn't recognize. No individual letters had been sent, but the time and place of the funeral had been announced in the newspapers. Snowdrifts still rose on either side of the road which I knew so well, and after a few miles' driving the sun began to shine.

The night before, when we were left alone in the living room while Isabel went to do some shopping, Mona had confided to me something that had struck me as very odd.

"I can say this to you now we're alone, Donald. . . . I keep wondering if Ray didn't do it on purpose. . . ."

I couldn't have been more astonished.

"You mean that he committed suicide?"

"That's not a word I like. . . . He may have decided to give fate a little push. . . ."

"Was he in trouble?"

"Not in business trouble. . . . As to that, he was more successful than he had ever expected."

"In his private life?"

"No, it wasn't that, either. . . . We were great friends, he and I. . . . He used to tell me everything. . . . Or almost everything. . . . There was nothing hidden between us. . . ."

The words surprised me. So there really were people who could look into one another's eyes and hide nothing. Was that what Isabel had been seeking for so many years in my eyes, a complete openness between us, a frank admission of everything that went on in my heart and in my mind?

"He had many affairs. . . . There was his secretary, the red-haired Hilda. . . .

"It's difficult to explain, Donald. . . . I wonder sometimes if he didn't envy you. . . ."

"Me?"

"You had studied together. . . . He could have been a lawyer. It was his ambition when he started in New York. . . . Then he became legal adviser in this publicity company. . . . He began to make money and realized that he could earn more that way. Can you understand what I mean? He had become a businessman. We had one of the most beautiful apartments on Sutton Place, and we entertained or were entertained every night. . . . In the end he was sick of it all."

"He told you so?"

"One night he had too much to drink and he admitted to me that one of these days he'd have had enough of playing the fool. . . . You know what happened to his father?"

Of course I did. I had known Herbert Sanders very well; I'd often spent the weekend with him when I went to Yale.

Ray's father was a book dealer, an odd sort of book dealer. He didn't have a business in town. He lived in a house in the best New England style, on Ansonia Road, and all the walls of the rooms on the ground floor were lined with books. People came to see him not only from New Haven but from Boston, New York, and farther afield, and he also did a lot of business by mail.

He corresponded all over the world, and kept abreast of everything that appeared in the fields of paleontology, archeology, and art, particularly prehistoric art. He had two other hobbies: works on Venice and books on gastronomy; he was the proud possessor of more than one hundred and sixty of such titles.

An odd man. I can see him now . . . youthful, aristocratic, with a smile that was at once encouraging and ironic.

His first wife, the mother of Ray and Bob, had left him to marry a rich Texas landowner. He had lived alone for several years and had acquired the reputation of being a skirt chaser. Then suddenly he married a Pole whom no one knew, a beautiful young woman of twenty-eight. He was fifty-five years old. Three months after his marriage, one evening when his wife was out, he shot himself through the head, surrounded by his books, leaving no letter, no explanation.

Mona repeated:

"Do you see what I mean?"

I refused to accept what she was telling me—I wanted Ray to be the man I had always imagined him to be, hard in his core and toward others, ambitious and cold, the strong man on whom I had taken revenge for all the strong men in the world. I didn't want a Ray who was fed up with money and success.

"You must be mistaken, Mona. I'm certain that Ray was happy. . . . When they've had a few drinks, people tend to be romantic."

She was watching me, wondering whether she should believe me or not.

"He was beginning to have enough of it all," she insisted; "that is why he started drinking. . . . I started drinking with him. . . ."

She added, hesitantly:

"I didn't dare drink here . . . because of Isabel. . . ."

She bit her lip, as though fearing that she had hurt me.

"You are afraid of Isabel?"

"Aren't you? Ray was, too. He admired you. . . ."

"Admired me?"

"He said you had chosen your life with your eyes wide open, wisely, that you had no need of artificial stimulation, that you'd no desire to be out every night running after the girls. . . ."

"Was he making fun of me?"

I was nonplused. The picture had changed completely.

"Ray said a man who could marry someone like Isabel, and live with her, year in, year out . . ."

"But why? Did he tell you why?"

"Don't you understand?"

She was surprised by my alertness, and I suddenly understood her attitude toward me in these last days. For her, I was the strong man, not Ray.

And quite naturally she had turned to me for protection. When, sitting in her armchair, she had watched me, when she had touched me with her shoulder, it had had nothing to do with sensuality.

"I have watched you both so often, Donald. With Isabel, it's not possible to cheat. It's impossible not to live up to her standard, even for a moment. She's an extraordinary woman; I think that to live with her you must be extraordinary, too."

This baffled me so completely that it took me two hours to get to sleep.

"Ray had his ups and downs, like everybody else. . . . You won't let me down, will you, now that he's gone?"

"But, Mona, on the contrary, all I ask . . ."

I got to my feet and was on the point of throwing myself on her and taking her in my arms. I was disturbed, exalted, beyond myself. . . .

"Sh! Here she is!"

We could see the small Volkswagen in the snow; I had given it to my wife for her local driving. I could see Isabel emerging from the garage, with her shopping bag in her hand, her face smooth, her complexion clear, always slightly pink on the cheekbones, and her blue eyes, those eyes that refused to permit lies, or even half-truths.

I had to re-examine the whole situation. Ray had admired me. It was the most staggering news.

Mona, too, admired me. She had just admitted it in her own way. And I was the poor idiot who had not dared to move my hand along the floor to touch the hand that had so desperately tempted me on that first night!

What Mona didn't know when she talked of my relationship with Isabel was that I was free of it now. I, too, had admired my wife. I had even been afraid of her, afraid of her frown, of a passing shadow in the limpid eyes, of the unspoken verdict.

Yet she had never said anything unpleasant to me. There had never been a single reproach. I must often have been unjust, unpleasant, ridiculous, who knows what else, toward her or our children.

Not a word. The smile never left her lips. There were only her eyes. And nobody would have seen anything in them. They remained limpid, serene.

What would Mona have thought if I had blurted out:

"It wasn't a woman I married, it was a judge."

Ray had surely been aware of this—surely he must have pitied me more than he had admired me? Or had he been mistaken all around?

He had believed that I was a strong man, and that I had married Isabel because I was strong enough to accept the challenge. In fact the opposite was the case. With Isabel I was still hiding in my mother's skirts. I had remained a boy scout. I had never stopped going to school. It didn't matter what Ray thought, I regretted nothing, beyond the fact that he had cheated me of my sense of guilt. I *wanted* to have killed him. I had willed his death, had assisted fate to the best of my ability.

If Ray had not even wanted to protect himself, if he had accepted death as a relief, the tragedy I had lived that night on the bench no longer had any meaning.

I wanted my revolt to be total, a decision of my own making. I wasn't meek and mild as people had believed. I was cruel, cynical, capable of letting my best friend die without lifting a finger. And while he was slowly going through the agony of dying in the snow on my land, with his leg twisted beneath him, I was smoking cigarettes and thinking of all the times he had humiliated me without knowing it. . . . And he wasn't the only one! . . . There was Isabel, too. The two images dissolved into one another in my mind. . . .

The funeral procession had to slow down two or three times. I tried to catch a glimpse of Mona's car, but there were several other cars between us now. Was I in love with her? I was able now to ask myself these questions completely frankly, without lying to myself, without cheating.

The answer was no. I didn't love her. If I could have married her tomorrow, I wouldn't have done so. Nor had I any desire to live with her day and night, to link her life with mine.

What I did want, what would happen soon, was to make love to her.

Without tenderness. Without passion. Who knows? Perhaps even standing, like Ray with Patricia at the Ashbridges'.

I wanted a female, just like that, in passing, and to me, Mona was female through and through.

We arrived at the cemetery. The cars drove through one avenue after another in this city of the dead until we reached a new part of it on the hill. There was snow everywhere. The trees were like Christmas trees. Nobody wore boots, and we shook the snow out of our shoes while the coffin was being carried to the graveside.

The clergyman was brief. There were no other speeches. The Miller brothers pushed their way through to the front because of the cameras, and when I reached Mona I put my hand under her elbow.

Bob Sanders noticed it at once. He is a head taller than I am, and he looked down at me with what seemed to me to be lofty contempt.

A few days before, this would have shamed me, left me dismayed. Today it left me indifferent. It was a matter of indifference to me, too, that my wife should glance at me with a certain surprise, for the daring of my gesture must have astonished her.

Everybody moved back to the cars. I walked beside Mona and continued to hold her arm as if she needed it, though she was perfectly calm. Bob Sanders caught up with us and, paying no attention to me, said to Mona:

"I've got to say good-by now. My plane leaves in less than two hours. If you need anything, if there are any formalities that have to be gone through—here's my address in Bonn. . . ."

He gave her a card which he had ready, and she slipped it into her handbag.

"Be brave, Mona."

He shook her hand in almost military fashion and hurried away. His car was the first to leave the cemetery.

"He didn't seem to like you."

He had not even said good-by to me. . . .

"No. I dare say he imagines things. . . ."

Isabel reached us.

"Are you driving alone to New York, Mona?"

"Yes—why not?"

"Won't it be very painful to go into the apartment alone?"

"My maid, Janet, will be expecting me."

Isabel glanced at me. It was almost as if she were telling me to go ahead. I could suggest accompanying Mona and coming back by train in the evening.

I didn't even ask her to come and have a bite with us. On the other hand, as I helped her into her Lincoln, I kissed her on both cheeks and held her for a second.

"Good-by, Mona. . . ."

"Good-by, Donald. Thank you. . . . I expect I'll have to ask you to help with the formalities, the will and I don't know what else. . . ."

"All you have to do is to call me at my office."

"Good-by, Isabel. . . . Thank you, too. . . . I don't know what I would have done without you."

They kissed each other. One of the Miller brothers came up to me as soon as Mona's car drove off.

"Are you her lawyer?"

"I guess so. . . ."

"There'll be some complicated business to settle. . . . Will you give me your telephone number?"

I gave him my card.

We were alone now, Isabel and I, in the Chrysler.

"Do you want to have some lunch on the way?"

"No, I'm not hungry."

"Neither am I."

I was at the wheel. She sat beside me, as usual, and in the right-hand corner of my field of vision I caught a glimpse of her profile.

After driving for a quarter of an hour in silence Isabel said very softly:

"What did you think of the ceremony?"

"The funeral?"

"Yes. . . . I don't know why, but I didn't feel at ease at all. . . . Somehow, there didn't seem to be any coherence or any order to it. I felt nothing. . . . I don't think anybody did, not even Mona. . . . Of course she really doesn't realize yet . . ."

I said nothing, lit a cigarette.

"It will be hardest when she gets home. . . ."

I remained silent. It was she, now, who seemed to want to break the silence.

"I wondered if you shouldn't have gone with her. . . ."

"She'll manage all right alone."

"Will you take on the business side?"

"She asked me to. And the Millers want to get in touch with me."

"Do you think she'll have enough to live on?"

"Certainly, I'm sure of that."

Was I strong? Was I weak? Was I deep? Was I naïve? Was I cruel? Was I a coward? They were all wanting to know. Even Isabel didn't know the answers and probably wondered why, after the business with the cigarette butts, I didn't appear more humble, if not plain scared.

Back at home, we simply had a sandwich in the kitchen. It was three o'clock.

"Are you going out?" I asked.

"Yes, I'll go out in a minute to do the shopping."

It seemed strange to me to find ourselves alone in the house. It had only been a few days, but I had lost the habit of it and wondered how we would get along now, just the two of us.

I went to the office. Higgins was waiting for me.

"I hope you're going to look after Sanders' will?"

"I'm certainly going to advise Mona Sanders, but in a private capacity. There'll be no question of a fee."

Higgins made a face.

"Pity. It must be quite an estate."

"I've no idea what it amounts to. . . . On the other hand it's quite likely the Miller brothers will ask me to liquidate the partnership, and that'll be a different matter. . . ."

"Everything went well?"

"The usual thing. . . ."

I could not have described everything that had happened at the cemetery for the good reason that I had been absorbed in my own thoughts, concerned only with Mona.

As soon as I got to the office, I was tempted to call her on the telephone and ask whether she had got back safely; I needed to hear her voice. Yet, I repeat, I wasn't in love. I know it's hard to understand, but perhaps I can make myself clear.

I worked for two solid hours on another estate. The dead man had taken such careful precautions to avoid paying taxes that it was almost impossible to establish any kind of estimate of his property and divide it between the heirs. I had been studying his file for several weeks.

I dictated a few letters to Helen, wondering why I

had never thought of making any advances to her before her marriage. I often looked at pretty girls, of course, including the wives of some of my friends. Sometimes I wanted them in a vague way. But that was as far as it went.

It was forbidden. By what? By whom? I had never asked myself the question.

I was married. There was Isabel with her clear blue eyes, her calm and easy personality.

Yes, Isabel and our daughters. I was fond of our daughters, Mildred and Cecilia, and when Mildred, the elder, left us for boarding school I missed going to kiss her good night in the evening.

Now, apart from two weekends a month, I had no reason to go up to their floor. Mildred was fifteen. If she married early, in three or four years, at the most in five, hers would be the first empty room in the house.

Then it would be Cecilia's turn, and time would pass more and more rapidly. For instance, the last five years had seemed to me much shorter than a single year between the ages of ten and twenty. Was it because they were less occupied? I dictated, and went on thinking at the same time. I watched Helen and wondered if she was already pregnant and, if she were, whom we would find to take her place. Ray went to bed with his secretary. He had gone to bed with all the women who came his way.

Yet it was he whom Mona was sorry for. He was disillusioned because he'd never found what he had hoped for in life. So he drank and ran after women. . . . Poor Ray! . . .

Was Helen aware that it was a new man sitting opposite her? And Higgins? Did all the people whom I was going to meet know they had another Donald Dodd to deal with now?

My gestures, the way I looked, hadn't changed. Neither had my voice. But what about my expression? How could my expression possibly be the same?

I went to stare at myself in the mirror of the washroom. My eyes are blue, too, a darker blue than Isabel's; they have a tinge of brown, while hers are really the color of a spring sky when the air is fresh and clear.

I taunted my reflection in the glass:

"How much better off are you going to be? How far has all this got you? . . . What exactly are your plans for the future?"

I have none. I shall just go on. I shall go to bed with Mona, certainly, without its being of any importance.

Saturday morning or Friday evening we'll go to fetch the girls at Litchfield, Isabel or I or both of us, presenting, in the car, the picture of a united family.

Except for the fact that I no longer believed in the family, I no longer believed in anything, neither in myself nor in anybody else. In fact I no longer believed in humanity itself and had begun to understand why Ray's father had killed himself.

Who knows whether the same thing might not happen to me one day? It was comforting to have a revolver in the night-table drawer.

The day might come when I would have had enough

of struggling in a vacuum . . . and then there would be a gesture and it would all be over.

Isabel would manage very well with the girls, and they would get quite a considerable sum from insurance.

Nobody could read these thoughts on my face. One gets so used to people that one continues to see them as one has always seen them. Did I, for instance, realize that Isabel was in her forties and that her hair was beginning to turn gray? It took an effort to convince myself that we had, both of us, passed the halfway mark in our lives and would soon be old.

Wasn't I already an old man in my daughters' eyes? Would the idea ever have occurred to them that I wanted to make love to a woman like Mona? It struck me they probably told each other that their mother and I no longer made love and that that was why they didn't have a swarm of brothers and sisters.

I went home and found Isabel cooking. Her head was lowered, and I touched her cheek with my lips as I always did; then I went to change my jacket for an old one I kept for the house, of soft tweed with elbows patched with leather. I opened the liquor cupboard and shouted:

"Will you have one?"

She knew what that meant.

"No, thanks. . . . Well, perhaps a little one."

I poured her a small Scotch and myself a stiff one. She joined me in the living room, wearing the print housecoat she usually wore when she was doing the household chores.

"I haven't changed yet."

I brought her her glass.

"Your good health!"

"And yours, Donald."

It seemed to me that her voice was intentionally grave, that it carried some message.

I chose not to look at her eyes, fearing that I might read in them something new and strange. I went and sat in my armchair in the library while she returned to what she was doing.

What had she thought when she had found the cigarette butts? When she went to the barn didn't she know that she was going to find them, that she was, in any case, going to find some trace of me?

What had made her suspect that, when I left the house to search for Ray, I had no intention of plunging into the blizzard? She hadn't seen me change direction—the night was too dark. She wouldn't have heard me shout because of the din.

I, myself, hadn't known in advance what I was going to do. It was only after I'd taken those first steps that I had decided to go another way.

Did she know that I was a coward? For originally it was just that. An insurmountable physical cowardice. I was at the end of my tether, and my one and only thought was to get out of the storm.

Could she have guessed it? It was only on the bench that I had realized that I was glad that Ray had disappeared, that he must be dead unless a miracle had returned him to the right path.

Had she understood all that? And in that case what

were her feelings toward me? Were they feelings of contempt? Of pity? There was nothing of either to be seen in her eyes. In fact there was only curiosity.

Another, more extravagant idea came to me. It had occurred to Olsen, which also explained some of his questions, but Olsen knew me only slightly and his way of thinking was that of a policeman.

Lieutenant Olsen had looked at Mona and myself in turn, asking himself if there was some bond between us. Of that I am certain. I could swear that he had done his research. Well, as luck would have it, at the Ashbridge party I had hardly ever been anywhere near Mona.

Does Isabel believe that Mona and I have secret meetings? I go to New York once a week, usually, and spend the day there. Sometimes I stay overnight. Ray was often away, for his agency has offices in Los Angeles and in Las Vegas.

When she saw me come back alone, did my wife have the idea, if only for a moment, that I had profited by the nightmare of the storm to rid myself of Ray?

Thinking of it cold-bloodedly, it doesn't seem impossible to me. I really believe that if she heard that I had killed someone, she wouldn't react any differently, she would go on living beside me, watching me, as she does now, with curiosity, hoping to understand me.

We ate, just the two of us, in the dining room, and the two silver candlesticks were on the table as usual, each with its two red candles. This was a tradition she had brought from her own home. Her father, the surgeon, had been rather fond of pomp and ceremony.

At my home, above the printing offices and the *Citizen,* life was far simpler. My father hadn't even telephoned me to ask for news of Ray's accident. Yet he went on editing his weekly paper at Torrington, one of the most ancient weeklies in New England, which had existed for more than a hundred years.

He had lived alone since my mother's death. He had resumed his bachelor's habits, and when he didn't eat in the restaurant opposite his house, he liked to prepare his meals himself. The woman who came to clean the offices every morning went up to the first floor to tidy up and make the bed.

We lived only about thirty miles from each other, but I didn't visit him more than once in every two or three months. I would walk into his glazed office where he always sat without his jacket, and he would raise his eyes from his papers, appearing to be surprised to see me.

"Good morning, son."

"Good morning, Dad."

He went on writing or correcting proofs, or telephoning. I would sit down in the only armchair in the room, which was in the same place as when I was a child.

"Everything all right?" he would ask finally.

"Yes."

"Isabel?"

He had a weakness for her, though he was a little afraid of her. He used to tell me now and then, joking: "You don't deserve a woman like that." To which he added always, for the sake of fairness:

"Any more than I deserved your mother."

She had died three years ago.

"Your girls?"

He was never certain about their age and thought they were younger than they were.

He was seventy-four years old. Tall and gaunt, and stooping. I had always seen him like that, with small malicious gray eyes.

"And the business?"

"I've no complaints. . . ."

He looked at the window.

"I see you have a new car."

He had had his for ten years. True, he didn't use it much. He was always in sole charge of the *Citizen* and his few helpers were indulgent.

A woman of about sixty, Mrs. Fuchs, whom I had known all my life, looked after the advertising side. My father printed visiting cards, announcements, brochures, and catalogues for local firms. He had never tried to expand his business; on the contrary, its activities declined slowly from year to year.

"What are you thinking about?"

I raised my head abruptly, as if caught napping, such is the force of habit.

"About my father. . . . I was saying to myself that he hasn't telephoned us."

Isabel no longer had her father and mother, only two brothers, both of whom lived in Boston, and a married sister in California.

"I must go and see him one of these mornings."

"It's more than a month since you've been there."

I promised myself that I would go to Torrington: the idea of going to see my father, and our house, with my new eyes, was very engaging.

I went back to the library, where I hesitated between my newspaper and television. I ended by opening the newspaper, and a quarter of an hour later, as I heard the hum of the dishwasher, Isabel joined me.

"Don't you think you ought to telephone Mona?"

Was it a trap? She seemed sincere, as usual. Would she in fact be capable of insincerity?

"Why should I?"

"You were Ray's best friend. She can't have many friends in New York, and Bob Sanders flew back without even staying another day. . . ."

"Bob is constituted that way. . . ."

"She'll be feeling lonely in that enormous apartment. Will she be able to keep up such a big place?"

"I don't know."

"Did Ray have money?"

"He earned a lot."

"He spent a lot, too, didn't he?"

"I believe so. His share in the Miller and Miller business must represent quite a tidy sum. . . ."

"When do you plan to go to see her?"

It wasn't an interrogation. She was talking quite simply and easily, as a wife talks to a husband.

"Do call her, please. . . . I'm sure it'll do her good. . . ."

I knew Ray's telephone number by heart, because I used to see him now and then on my trips to New York.

I dialed it and listened to the ringing that went on for quite a time.

"There seems to be no one there."

"Unless she's in the tub. . . ."

Just then I heard Mona's voice:

"Hello. Who is speaking?"

"Donald."

"It's sweet of you to call, Donald. . . . If you only knew how lost I feel here, all alone. . . ."

"That's why I'm calling. . . . It was Isabel's idea."

"Do thank her for me. . . ."

I thought I could detect some irony in her voice.

"If you weren't so far away I would have asked you to come and spend the evening with me. . . . My faithful Janet does what she can. . . . I just pace up and down the rooms; I don't know what to do with myself. . . . Have you ever felt like that?"

"No. . . ."

"Lucky you. . . . The business this morning was dreadful. . . . That endless procession and all those people, at the cemetery . . . If you hadn't been there . . ."

So she had noticed that I had held her arm.

"I was just about ready to faint from sheer exhaustion. And that big oaf of a Bob saying good-by so ceremoniously and then rushing off to the airport."

"Yes, I know. . . ."

"Did the Millers speak to you?"

"They asked me if I was going to be looking after your business affairs. . . ."

"What did you tell them?"

"That I'd help you as much as I could. . . . You do understand, Mona, I don't want to impose myself in any way. . . . I'm only a small-town lawyer. . . ."

"Ray considered you a lawyer of first-rate ability!"

"There are plenty of them in New York far more experienced than I am."

"I want it to be you. . . . Unless Isabel . . ."

"No. . . . She wouldn't have any objection to it . . . quite the contrary."

"Are you free on Monday?"

"At what time?"

"Any time you say. . . . It will take you two hours to get here. Would eleven o'clock be all right?"

"I'll be there."

"Now I'll do what I wanted to do at five o'clock this afternoon: swallow two sleeping pills and lie down. If I could just sleep for forty-eight hours . . ."

"Good night, Mona."

"Good night, Donald. . . . Till Monday. Thank Isabel for me again."

"I'll do it at once."

I hung up.

"Mona thanks you."

"What for?"

"First of all, for all that you did for her. Secondly, for letting me take on the estate."

"What reason could I have had to oppose it? Have I ever stopped you in anything to do with business?"

It was true. I was compelled to laugh. It wasn't her way. She never allowed herself to give advice. At the most, very rarely, under certain circumstances, she would give an approving glance, or on the other hand her expression would go blank, which was a warning in itself.

"You're going to New York on Monday?"

"Yes."

"By car?"

"It will depend on the weather forecast. If they talk of more snow, I'll take the early train."

There it was. It was easy. We were talking calmly like an ordinary couple, using ordinary words. People listening to us or seeing us would have taken us for a model couple. Yet Isabel considered me a coward or a murderer, I don't know which. And I had decided that I would sleep with Mona, this coming Monday.

The house had its familiar purr, for it was a lived-in house; it was very old and had sheltered many human lives. The rooms had grown larger, with time, windows had been transformed into doors. Walls had been put up and other walls had been taken down. Scarcely twenty feet from the bedroom, there was a swimming pool dug out of the rock.

The house breathed. From time to time we could hear the furnace in the cellar going on. Then a noise might come from one of the radiators or from the paneling, or one of the beams creaked. Up until December we had had a cricket in the chimney.

Isabel unfolded her paper and wiped her glasses, for she had taken to reading glasses in the last few years. It gave her different eyes, less sure of themselves, less limpid, almost afraid.

"Is Higgins well?"

"Yes, very well."

"Has his wife recovered from her flu?"

"I didn't ask him."

Gently we were allowing ourselves to be ensnared for the rest of the evening; I had lived like that for seventeen years.

V

It happened, as I had expected it to, and I don't think that Mona was surprised. I'm even almost certain that she expected it, that she anticipated it, which doesn't mean that she was in love with me.

Before it happened we had the traditional weekend with our daughters. We went together to meet them at Litchfield, Isabel and I, and we couldn't avoid the quarter of an hour's conversation with Mrs. Jenkins, who has small, black, sparkling eyes and spits when she talks.

"If all our pupils were like your Mildred . . ."

On the whole I hate schools and especially the occasions when parents are reunited with their children. First of all, one relives one's own life and all its various stages, which is in itself embarrassing. Then one thinks back to the first pregnancy, the baby's first cry, its first tooth, and finally the day one took the child to its first school and returned alone.

The years are marked by milestones, by the prize givings, the holidays. Traditions are established which one believes to be immutable. Another child is born, who goes through the same rites and gets the same teachers. And then one finds oneself with a girl of fifteen, another one of twelve, and one has become a man in his decline. As in Tommy Brown's song, there are the bells of baptism, the marriage bells, the bells of the funeral. Then new lives come into being and it begins all over again.

Mildred's first question when she got into the car was:

"Can I go and spend the night with Sonia, Mummy?"

They always ask for permission from their mother, as if I didn't exist. Sonia is the daughter of Charles Brawton, a neighbor who is a sort of friend of ours.

"Has she asked you?"

"Yes. They're having a little party at their house, and she wants me to spend the night with her."

Mildred has a face that makes you want to eat her up, it's so delectable. Her skin is clear, like her mother's, but freckled on the nose and under the eyes. It distresses her —she doesn't know that that's part of her charm. Her features are still rather childish, and so is her figure, which resembles a doll's.

"What do you think, Donald?"

I must admit that Isabel always consults me. But had I made the mistake of refusing, it would set the children against me, so that I always said yes.

"And what about me!" exclaimed Cecilia. "Am I to stay at home alone?"

For to be with us means being alone. People talk about

family, about the closeness between parents and children! Cecilia is twelve, and already she talks in terms of solitude.

That is as it should be. I was the same at her age. I remember the grim, interminable Sundays with my parents, particularly when it rained.

"We'll ask one of your friends."

And the parents telephone and organize exchanges.

"Could Mabel come and spend the weekend with us?"

On Sunday at eleven o'clock the four of us went together to church. There, too, one sees people grow older, year after year.

"Is it true that your friend Ray died in our garden?"

"Yes, darling."

"Will you show me the spot?"

We didn't show it to her. With children one pretends that death doesn't exist, as if only the others, the strangers, the people who don't belong to the family or the little circle of friends, pass from life to death.

Never mind. All this is unimportant. What is more perplexing is that Cecilia suddenly said, as we were having breakfast on Sunday:

"Are you sad, Mummy?"

"No . . . no, I'm not sad."

"Is it because of what happened to Ray?"

"No, my darling, I'm as usual. . . ."

The two girls resemble Isabel more than they do me, but Cecilia has something different. Her hair is almost chestnut-colored, her pupils are like nuts, and even when she was quite small she made remarks that surprised us.

She must be very deep and have an inner life of which we have no knowledge.

"Are you both taking us back?"

"Ask your father."

I said yes. We took them back on Sunday night, having in fact hardly seen them. I had watched television; I would be hard put to say what Isabel had been doing. She is always busy. Our cleaning woman has resumed her work. Her surname is Dawling. Her husband is the village drunk, a true, inveterate drunk who fights in bars every Saturday and who is found sleeping on the sidewalk or by the side of the road.

He has tried many jobs and been dismissed everywhere. Lately he has been raising pigs, in a pen he built with old boards at the end of his land. The local council try to stop him, because everybody complains.

They have eight children, all boys, who resemble their father and are the terror of the neighborhood. People call them the Hooligans, without distinguishing them one from another, and they usually go in pairs, for Mrs. Dawling almost always gives birth to twins.

These people form a gang, a clan, that lives outside the community, into which only poor Mrs. Dawling is admitted to help and clean. She rarely talks to me. Her lips are thin, and she looks at the world with contempt. She is willing to serve, but this doesn't prevent her from having her own opinions.

"Do you think you'll be spending the night in New York? Do you want me to pack your suitcase?"

"No. . . . I'll surely be through by the evening."

Her expression begins to irritate me. I no longer know exactly what it means. It isn't ironical, yet it seems to say:

"I know all about you, my boy. Everything. You can do what you want, but don't think you're hiding anything from me."

In a perverse kind of way, the expression contains some curiosity, as if, all the time, she is wondering how I'm going to react, what I'm going to do.

She has a new man before her, and perhaps she feels she hasn't explored all his possibilities. She knows I'm going to New York to see Mona. Had she felt, while Mona was here, that I desired her? Does she suspect what is going to happen? She is very careful not to show any jealousy. It was she, Thursday night, who suggested that I should telephone to Sutton Place, she who on Sunday evening asked me if I wanted my suitcase, as if it were understood that I would spend the night in New York.

Sometimes I wonder if she's not actually pushing me. But why? To avoid any revolt on my part? To safeguard what is still there to safeguard?

She knows very well that in the last week we have become strangers. Strangers who live together, who eat at the same table, undress in front of one another, and sleep in the same room. Strangers who talk together as husband and wife. Would I still be capable of making love to her? I don't think so.

Why? Something had snapped when I was sitting on the red bench in the barn, smoking cigarettes.

Mona has nothing to do with it, whatever Isabel may think.

The sky was dark on Sunday night. I announced: "I'm taking the train. . . ."

I got up at six o'clock on Monday. The sky was brighter but it seemed to me that the air smelled of snow.

"Would you like me to drive you to the station?"

She drove me in the Chrysler. The Millerton station is a small wooden building where there are never more than three or four people waiting for the train, a train in which everyone knows everyone else, at least by sight. Our shoemaker, who was also going to New York, greeted me.

"It isn't worth-while waiting. . . . You might as well go home. . . . I'll call and tell you which train I'm catching back. . . ."

It didn't snow. On the contrary. As we approached New York, the weather cleared, and the skyline stood out against a nearly perfect blue, flecked by a few golden clouds.

I first went to have some coffee. It was too early to go to Mona's, and when I left the station I walked along Park Avenue. There was no reason why I, too, shouldn't live in New York, have an office in one of these glass buildings, lunch with clients or friends, have a drink at the end of the day, in an intimate, dark little bar. We would be able to go to theaters in the evening or to dance in a night club. . . .

We could . . .

What exactly was it that Mona had said on this subject? That Ray envied me, that I was the stronger of the two, that I had made my choice wisely. Ray, who had been successful in everything and talked of putting a bullet through his head. What stupidity!

Were passers-by really looking at me? I've always had the impression that people have been looking at me as if I had a spot in the middle of my face or as if I were wearing some ridiculous clothes. It has been such a strong feeling that when I was a child, and later when I was a young man, I would stop in front of the shop-windows to reassure myself that there was nothing abnormal about my appearance.

At half past ten I hailed a taxi and told the driver to go to Sutton Place. I knew the apartment house, the orange marquee, the uniformed doorman, the hall with its leather armchairs and, to the right, the receptionist.

He knew me, too.

"Is it for Mrs. Sanders, Mr. Dodd? . . . Shall I announce you?"

"No, it isn't necessary. She's expecting me. . . ."

The elevator man wore white cotton gloves. He stopped at the twenty-first floor, and I knew at which of the three mahogany doors I should ring.

Janet came to let me in. She is a delectable girl in her black silk uniform, a pretty embroidered apron, and usually with a smile on her face.

I suppose she felt she ought to make some kind of face suitable to the circumstances and murmured something like

"Who would have believed . . ."

Taking off my coat and hat, I let myself be led into the living room, which every time I see it gives me a feeling of giddiness. It is a vast room, painted white, and looks out over the East River. I had known Ray long enough to be aware that he hadn't chosen the décor to suit his own taste. The room was a challenge, a sort of window dressing. He wanted to appear rich, modern, dazzling. The furniture, the pictures on the wall, the sculpture on the pedestals, seemed to have been chosen for a movie set rather than to be lived with, and the vastness of the room excluded all idea of intimacy.

A door opened out of a little room they called the boudoir, and Mona called out to me:

"Come in here, Donald."

I hesitated whether to take my brief case. Finally I left it on the armchair. I walked toward her. There were about thirty feet between us. She stood in the doorway, dressed in dark blue. She waited, watching me approaching.

She let me pass without giving me her hand, then she closed the door behind me.

Only then did we look into each other's eyes, face to face.

I put my hands on her shoulders and began to kiss her on the cheeks, as I had done when Ray was alive. Then suddenly I put my lips to hers, holding her body close to mine.

She didn't protest, didn't stiffen. I could see her eyes, which were fixed on me with a kind of astonishment. Hadn't she known that this was going to happen? Was she surprised that it had happened so quickly? Or was it my excitement, my clumsiness, that surprised her? My whole body was trembling.

In my heart of hearts I wanted to cry.

The blue housecoat was of a very fine silk, and I felt she had nothing underneath it. Was it on purpose? Had she not had time to dress because I had come ten minutes earlier than expected?

I murmured:

"Mona. . . ."

And she said to me:

"Come. . . ."

We remained in each other's arms and she moved with me toward a sofa; we tumbled onto it at the same time.

I literally dived into her, suddenly, violently, almost cruelly, and for the space of a second there was fear in her eyes.

When I rose, she quickly got up, too, tying the belt of the gown.

"Forgive me, Mona. . . ."

"Why should I forgive you?"

She smiled at me, with some joy left in her eyes, but it was a smile not without melancholy.

I confessed:

"I wanted it so much!"

"I know. What is your drink, Donald?"

There was a small bar concealed in a Louis XV piece of furniture. There was no question of hiding the huge bar in the living room.

"The same as yours."

"Then it will be Scotch. Did Isabel say anything?"

"About what?"

"About your coming to see me."

"On the contrary. It was her idea."

It was a curious sensation, which I had never experienced before. We had just made love, savagely, and you could see it still on Mona's face. Perhaps you could see it on mine, too. Yet, as soon as we were on our feet again, we were both talking like old friends. We were very much at our ease, both in body and mind. My eyes must have been laughing.

"To us, Donald."

"To us. . . ."

"What a strange woman she is. . . . She intimidates me very much. . . . But then it is true that for a long time you intimidated me, too. . . ."

"I did?"

"Does it surprise you? With most people you know

which way to take them. You can detect their weak spots immediately. But you, you have no weak spots."

"You've just had proof that I have. . . ."

"You call that a weak spot?"

"Perhaps it is. You know, that night when we slept on mattresses on the floor, I was hypnotized by your hand lying on the floor. I had an insane desire to touch it, to seize it. . . . I wonder what would have happened if I had done it. . . ."

"With Isabel there?"

"With the whole world watching, as far as I cared. . . . Don't you call that a weak spot?"

She seemed to consider it for a moment as she sat in an armchair. The housecoat had slipped, uncovering almost the whole of her thigh, but it didn't embarrass either of us. We paid no attention to it.

"No," she ended by saying.

"Was it too sudden . . . did I shock you?"

"Yes, I admit I was surprised. . . ."

We were able to talk about it quite simply, without romanticism, like two good friends, like accomplices who admit their weaknesses to one another.

"We had to do it or we would have spent a ridiculous day, and I shouldn't have been able to think of anything else. . . ."

"You like me a little, Donald, do you?"

"I like you a lot."

"I'll need it. I don't want to play the distressed widow, and besides it would be in bad taste just now. . . . I liked Ray very much, you know that. . . . We were friends."

I was sitting in front of her, and here too the bay window overlooked the East River.

"When I came home on Thursday, I almost called you. The apartment seemed ten times as big as it really is, and I felt lost in it. I paced up and down, touched the furniture, the little ornaments, as if to make sure they were really there. . . . I poured myself a drink, then another one. . . . When you called me that night, couldn't you tell from my voice that I had been drinking?"

"I was too excited to notice anything. . . . Isabel was watching me. . . ."

She too was watching me, silently at first, and then she said:

"I'll never be able to understand her. . . ."

She was smoking in a pensive way.

"Do you understand her?"

"No. . . ."

"Do you think she can suffer, that anything could upset that calm?"

"I don't know, Mona. . . . I've lived for seventeen years without asking myself that question. . . ."

"And now?"

"I've been asking it for a whole week."

"Doesn't she frighten you a little?"

"I was used to it. . . . It seemed quite simple. . . ."

"You don't believe that any more?"

"She watches me live and breathe, she knows my slightest reaction and no doubt my most trivial thought . . . but she never says a word that would suggest she knows anything. She remains calm and serene."

"Even now?"

"Why do you ask that?"

"Because she has understood. . . . A woman always does."

"Understood what?"

"That what happened just now was bound to happen. You were talking of the night we spent on the mattresses. . . . She did it on purpose, putting you beside me. . . ."

"So as not to appear to be jealous?"

"No . . . to test you. It's even more subtle than that, I'd swear it was. . . . To tempt you. . . . To startle your imagination. . . ."

I tried to understand, to see Isabel in the new role.

"She maneuvered it so we were alone at least twice, and she must have sensed my desire to feel your arms around me. . . . I needed comfort, I wanted to feel something solid beside me."

"Did I help you at all?"

"No. At first I thought you were afraid of her."

It wasn't the right word. I was never afraid of Isabel. Only afraid of hurting her, of disappointing her, of proving myself inferior to the image she had built up of me.

While my mother was alive I was afraid to upset her, and even now, if I feel uneasy in my father's printing office, in Torrington, it is because I don't want to feel I'm sorry for him.

He is only the shadow of his former self, as they say. He keeps up a front, out of bravado, and continues publishing his weekly, which by now hasn't even got a thousand subscribers. He continues his show of irony, which was his act all through his life, but he knows perfectly well that any day he'll have to be taken to the hospital, if he doesn't die suddenly in his bed or in his study. Can I let him see my anxiety? Or that every time I leave him I ask myself whether it has been the last time?

Mona glanced at a gilt clock.

"I could swear that at this very moment she knows what has happened."

She kept going back to Isabel, who obviously intrigued her, and I wondered why.

With someone else, I might have thought that she hoped I would get a divorce and marry her. This idea dismayed me somehow, and I rose to fill the glasses.

"Were you shocked by what I said, Donald?"

"No."

"You still love her, don't you?"

"No."

"But you did love her deeply at one time?"

"I don't think so."

She was drinking her Scotch in smaller gulps now, watching me all the while.

"I want to kiss you," she murmured at last, getting to her feet.

I got up too. I put my arm around her, and instead of kissing her on the lips I pressed my cheek against hers, and that is how we stood for a long time, looking at the view from the window.

I felt very sad.

Then this sadness transformed itself into a much sweeter emotion, with only a tinge of bitterness left. Pulling away from me, she said:

"I'd better dress before lunch."

I watched her going toward what I knew was the bedroom and resigned myself to sitting and reading a newspaper while I waited for her. My disappointment must have shown on my face, because she added, quite naturally:

"If you want to come along . . ."

I followed her to the room; one of the beds had been slept in. The door to the bathroom was open, and some water splashed on the tiled floor indicated that she had had her bath shortly before I arrived. She sat down at her dressing table and began to brush her hair before making up.

I followed her movements, the reflections of light on her skin, with a feeling of unaccountable bliss. I knew we had just made love, but it meant almost more to be accepted like this in her feminine intimacy.

"You amuse me, Donald."

"Why?"

"You look as if you were watching a woman dress for the first time in your life."

"It's true."

"But Isabel . . ."

"It isn't the same thing."

I had rarely seen Isabel sitting at her dressing table, which, anyway, had only the barest essentials, instead of all the little jars and bottles which I saw on Mona's.

"Would it bore you to have lunch with me here? I asked Janet to prepare a little meal for us. . . ."

I remembered two young lions in the Zoo that rolled about playfully together, in total confidence. The feeling I was now experiencing with Mona was much like that.

When she got up it was to look for some underwear, in her closet. She didn't leave the room to take off her housecoat, and she wasn't provocative either when she appeared naked. She dressed in the same natural way, as if she were alone, and I watched every gesture, every attitude.

Was it still true that I wasn't in love with her? I think it was. It never occurred to me to live with her, to merge our fate, as I had once done with Isabel.

I could see Ray's bed not slept in, and it didn't embarrass me, didn't evoke any unpleasant image. I knew there were two other bedrooms in the apartment. One night I had slept in one of them, because I had missed the train. Janet used the other one, a smaller one and nearer to the kitchen.

Strangely enough, there was no dining room, probably because all the space had gone into the living room.

"Am I all right? Not overdressed?"

She had chosen a dress of fine black wool, brightened by a silver belt. She must have known that black suited her.

"You look perfect, Mona."

"We'll have to have a serious talk soon. . . . I don't know what I would do without you, with all the problems ahead of me."

Janet had set a little table near one of the bay windows, and there was a tall bottle of Rhine wine in a bucket of ice.

"I must move, find a smaller apartment. . . . Actually, neither Ray nor I liked this one. For Ray it was a kind of window dressing. He wanted to impress his clients. He loved to entertain, you know, to have lots of people around him and watch them manipulating each other and see them when they loosened up. . . ."

She looked at me suddenly very earnestly.

"Do you know, I've never seen you drunk, Donald."

"But I have been drunk when you've been around. . . . Saturday evening at the Ashbridges', for instance. . . ."

"You were drunk?"

"Didn't you notice?"

She hesitated.

"Not at the time."

"When, then?"

"I don't know. . . . I'm not sure. . . . Forgive me

if I'm wrong. . . . When you came back after searching for Ray, you looked strange. . . ."

There was a cold lobster, *foie gras,* and some cold meat set on a side table so we could serve ourselves. I felt a rush of blood to my head.

"That wasn't drunkenness," I said.

"What was it, then?"

The die was cast. My mind was made up. There was no going back on it.

"The truth is that I didn't go to search for Ray. I was too exhausted. I couldn't breathe in the storm, and every minute I thought I'd have a heart attack. There was no chance of finding him in the dark, with the snow whipping my face and getting in my eyes. So I went to the barn. . . ."

She had stopped eating and was looking at me with such astonishment that I almost regretted my frankness.

"In the barn I sat on a bench that is stored there for the winter, and I lit a cigarette."

"You stayed there all the time?"

"Yes. . . . The cigarette butts were on the ground at my feet. . . . I smoked at least ten. . . ."

She was disturbed, but she showed no signs of resentment.

Finally she reached out for my hand and said:

"Thank you, Donald."

"For what?"

"For being frank. . . . For telling me the truth. . . . I felt that something had happened, but I didn't know what. . . . For a moment I even wondered whether you had a fight with Ray. . . ."

"Why should I have a fight with him?"

"Because of that woman. . . ."

"What woman are you talking about?"

"Mrs. Ashbridge. . . . Patricia. . . . When Ray and she went upstairs together, you seemed somehow upset. . . ."

I was astonished to find that she knew about that. . . .

"Did you see them too?"

"Just as they were leaving the room. . . . I hadn't followed them. . . . It was quite by chance that I saw them at all. . . . You weren't jealous of Ray?"

"Not because of her. . . ."

"Because of me?"

She was asking the question without any coyness. We were both quite relaxed. It wasn't, as with Isabel, a hidden battle.

"Because of everything. . . . I had actually pushed the door open, the one you saw them leave by. . . . I wasn't thinking of anything. . . . I had drunk more than usual. . . . I took them by surprise. . . . Then, suddenly, the way blood rushes to your head, I was shaken by a terrible jealousy. . . . At Yale I was a top student. Everyone thought I was much more brilliant than Ray. When he decided to establish himself in New York, I told him that it would be tough going, that he might get stuck. But it was I who buried myself in Brentwood, less than thirty miles from my father's house, as if I were afraid of the risk of striking out in a new direction. . . . And I married Isabel soon after, I suppose for even greater protection."

She listened to me, dismayed, raising her glass, pointing to mine. . . .

"Drink."

"I've told you everything now. . . . You can guess the rest, all the other things that went through my mind that Saturday. . . . Ray had got you, he had become a partner in Miller and Miller's, and all along the line he could pick women like Patricia . . . quite casually."

She murmured slowly:

"And it was he who envied you!"

"Am I disappointing you, Mona?"

"On the contrary."

She was moved. Her upper lip trembled.

"How did you have the courage to tell me all this?"

"You're the only person to whom I can talk. . . ."

"You hated Ray, didn't you?"

"That night, on my bench—yes, I did."

"And before that?"

"I thought of him as my best friend. . . . But, again on my bench, I discovered that I had been lying to myself."

"If you could have saved him. . . ?"

"I don't know. Probably I'd have done it, reluctantly. . . . I'm not sure of anything any more, Mona. . . . You see, during one night, I changed so much. . . ."

"I noticed it. . . . So did Isabel. . . ."

"She guessed so accurately that she went to the barn and found the cigarette butts."

"Did she tell you she did that?"

"No. . . . She destroyed them, I'm sure, because she was afraid that Lieutenant Olsen would discover them. . . ."

"Does Isabel believe that you . . . that you did something else?"

I chose to speak crudely.

"That I pushed Ray over the rock? I don't know. . . . All through last week she has been looking at me as if she didn't recognize me, as though she was trying to understand. You do understand, don't you?"

"I think so. . . ."

"Does it disappoint you?"

"No, Donald, just the opposite."

It was the first time I ever felt I was basking in a woman's warm regard.

"I wondered if you would talk to me about it. . . . I would have been a little sad if you hadn't. . . . It needed a lot of courage."

"From where I stand, you know . . ."

"Where do you stand?"

"It's as if I had blotted out seventeen years, or rather forty-five years of my life. Everything is in the past. . . . Yesterday, with the girls, I was ashamed, because I felt like a stranger. . . . But I will go on making the same gestures, saying the same things. . . ."

"Is it necessary?"

I looked at her. I hesitated. It would have been easy. Since I had blotted out everything, hadn't I the right to begin in a different way? Mona was there, facing me, grave, trembling.

The moment was crucial. We were eating, drinking Rhine wine, we looked out over the East River.

"Yes," I murmured. "It is necessary."

I don't know why. The "yes" came out hoarsely. I was looking at her intensely. I very nearly . . . No, not quite, but very soon I might have started to love her. I could also have established myself in New York. We could have . . . I don't know whether she was hurt. She didn't show it.

"Thank you, Donald. . . ."

She got up, brushed the crumbs off her dress.

"Will you have some coffee?"

"Yes, please."

She rang for Janet.

"Where would you like to have it? Here or in the boudoir?"

"In the boudoir."

This time I took my brief case with me. I walked slowly beside her, my hand on her shoulder.

"You understand, Mona, don't you? You know it wouldn't work. . . ."

She raised her hand to clasp mine, and I could see again that hand on the floor of our living room, lit by the flames from the fireplace.

I felt at ease, relaxed. A little later I sat down in front

of a small antique table on which I spread some paper and a pencil.

"First of all, do you know how you stand?"

"No, I know nothing. . . . Ray never spoke to me about his business affairs. . . ."

"Do you have some cash to tide you over?"

"We have a joint account at the bank."

"Do you know how much is in it?"

"No. . . ."

"Did Ray carry life insurance?"

"Yes. . . ."

"Do you know what arrangement he had with the Millers?"

"He was their partner, but not an equal partner, I believe. His share was increased annually."

"He left no will?"

"Not to my knowledge."

"Have you looked through his papers?"

"Yes. . . ."

I went with her to the study Ray had arranged for himself, and we went through his papers together. There was no uneasiness between us, no reservations.

The insurance policy, in Mona's name, was for two hundred thousand dollars.

"Have you informed the company?"

"Not yet."

"Nor the bank?"

"No. I've hardly left the house since Thursday. I went

out only once on Sunday morning for a stroll and to get some air."

"May I use your telephone?"

I was back in my role as lawyer and counselor. She heard me telephoning, surprised that everything could be settled so easily.

"Do you want me to go and see the Miller brothers in your name?"

"Yes, please, will you do that?"

I telephoned the Millers and announced my visit.

"I'll be back shortly," I said to Mona.

I took my brief case with me. In the living room I turned to her and very naturally, as I had expected, she came into my arms and kissed me.

The offices of the Miller brothers occupied two whole floors in one of the new buildings on Madison Avenue near the Cardinal's grayish residence. There were more than fifty employees working in one huge room alone, each at his desk, with one or two telephones, and I had a glimpse of the same anthill in the art department.

Both of them were waiting for me, David and Bill, short and corpulent, so much alike that people who didn't know them well couldn't tell them apart.

"We are glad that Mrs. Sanders has chosen you to represent her, Mr. Dodd. If she hadn't done so we would have picked you ourselves, as I told you at the cemetery."

The office was large, enveloping, just solemn enough for such serious business.

"What may I offer you? Scotch?"

A mahogany screen concealed a bar.

"I suppose that you have a general idea of the situation. Here is our partnership agreement as it was established five years ago."

It consisted of about ten pages, which I skimmed through. At a glance, Ray's share in the business could be estimated at about half a million dollars.

"Here are the last accountings. . . . You'll have time to study the documents at leisure and get in touch with us again. . . . When do you go back to Brentwood?"

"Probably tomorrow. . . ."

"Could we have lunch together?"

"I'll telephone you in the morning."

"Before you go, I would like you to take a look at the office of our poor friend to see if there are any papers or personal articles to take away."

Ray's office was almost as large the one I had left, and his beautiful red-haired secretary was working at a table. She rose to shake my hand, though I got the impression that she didn't greatly appreciate my visit. I knew her, because I'd come several times to meet Ray in his office.

"Do you know, Miss Tyler, whether Ray kept any personal papers here?"

"It depends what you call personal. . . . Perhaps you could tell. . . ."

She opened the file cabinets and let me look through the

folders. On the desk stood Mona's photograph in a silver frame.

"Perhaps I ought to take that with me?"

"I suppose so. . . ."

"I'll be back tomorrow. Would you be so kind as to put all these small things together for me?"

"There is even a coat in the closet."

"Thank you. . . ."

I rode to the bank, then to the insurance company. I was liquidating not only a man's past, but the man himself. I was proceeding to delete him legally, just as the Miller brothers were deleting him from their name plate . . .

It was six o'clock when I got back to Sutton Place. Mona opened the door, and we kissed as though it had become a rite.

"Not too tired?"

"No. . . . There's still a lot to do tomorrow. It would be better if you came with me to the Millers'."

Without asking me anything, she poured our drinks.

"Where would you like to . . ."

She was going to ask me again whether I preferred the living room or the boudoir.

"You know very well. . . ."

We began to drink, both of us, without talking much.

"My darling Mona, you are a rich woman. . . . With the insurance, the estate should amount to about seven hundred thousand dollars."

"As much as that?"

The sum surprised her, but one sensed that it hadn't any precise significance for her.

"May I call up my home?"

Isabel answered at once.

"You were right. . . . I can't possibly get back to Brentwood tonight. I've seen the Millers, yes, and I have to study the documents they gave me before tomorrow. . . ."

"Are you at Mona's?"

"Yes, I've just come back here."

"Will you spend the night at the Algonquin?"

This is where we usually stay when we spend the night in New York. It's near the theaters, and I was eight years old when I first stayed there with my father.

"I don't know yet."

"I see."

"Everything all right at home?"

"As usual. Nothing new."

"Good night, Isabel."

"Good night, Donald. . . . My love to Mona."

I repeated in an undertone, turning to Mona:

"My wife sends you her love."

"Thank her and give her mine."

When I hung up, she looked at me, a question in her eyes.

I realized that she was thinking of the Algonquin.

"Because of Janet . . ." I murmured.

"You imagine she doesn't know already?"

Her eyes turned to the sofa.

"Why shouldn't we go and dine in some small restaurant and then come back here to sleep?"

She filled our glasses.

"I must try to drink less. . . . I drink much too much, Donald."

Then, after a moment's thought, as though the idea had just struck her:

"You're not afraid that Isabel might call the Algonquin?"

I replied with a smile:

"Do you think she doesn't know already, too?"

I wondered if I would have to sleep in Ray's bed. As it turned out, there was room for both of us in Mona's bed, next to the empty one.

Part Two

I

Isabel continues to watch me. Nothing else. She asks no questions. There are no reproaches. She doesn't cry. She doesn't put on the air of a martyr. Life goes on unchanged. We sleep in the same room, use the same bathroom, eat facing each other across the same table, and in the evening, when I haven't brought any work home, we read or watch television.

The girls come for the usual weekend, every fortnight, and I don't think they notice any change. True, they are more preoccupied with their own personal lives than with ours.

Deep down, they're no longer interested in us, at least it's true of Mildred. The brother of one of her friends, who is twenty, is far more important to her than we are.

Every day, morning, noon, and night, Isabel looks at me with her pale blue eyes, which I seem all the time to collide with, and I end up, as usual, wondering what they are saying. Is there a message there? That's what I sometimes ask myself:

". . . Watch out, Donald dear. . . ."

No, they haven't enough warmth for that.

"If you imagine that I don't understand what's going on . . ."

Certainly she wants to show me she's perceptive, that nothing escapes her, has ever escaped her.

"You're going through a phase; most men at your age have to go through it."

If that's what she thinks, she's wrong. I know myself. I'm not experiencing the love agony of an aging man. Besides, I'm not in love. Neither do I indulge in unhealthy sexuality, I keep in control, aware of everything that goes on inside me and around me, and I am the only one to know that there is nothing new in my obscure thoughts, except that I finally allowed them to come up into the daylight and can look them in the face.

So what are these eyes trying to say?

"I'm sorry for you. . . ."

That is more plausible. There's always been in her the wish to protect me or to appear to be protecting me, just as she imagines she is protecting our daughters, or animating all the charitable activities to which she devotes so much of her time.

Modest and self-effacing, she actually is the most ambitious woman I've ever met. She never lets one see a single crack in her composure, the slightest sign of any of the normal little human weaknesses.

"I'll always be there, Donald."

There is this, too, in her eyes: the loyal companion sacrificing herself to the bitter end!

At the very bottom there is something else as well.

"You imagine you've set yourself free. . . . You believe you're a different man. . . . But you're still the same little boy that needs me, and you'll never get away. . . ."

I can't really tell. Sometimes I tend toward one hypothesis, sometimes toward another. I live like a microbe under the microscope of her eye, and there are times when I hate her.

Three months have passed since the night of the bench in the barn. The bench is no longer there, it is back in its place in the garden, at the bottom of the rock, right at the spot where Ray slipped. The last patches of snow have been sucked in by the warm soil and the daffodils are beginning to come up in yellow clumps.

The first month, I went to New York as often as twice a week, staying overnight almost every time, for Ray's estate, and the formalities it involved, required a lot of time and careful maneuvering.

"Where can I reach you if I have something urgent to tell you in the evening?"

"At Mona's."

I conceal nothing. Rather, I behave with a certain ostentation, and when I return from New York it gives me pleasure to detect some of Mona's scent on my skin.

Bad weather hasn't forced me to take the train again. I drive the whole way. There is a parking place opposite her house. Or rather there was one, for Mona left Sutton Place a fortnight ago.

Through some friends she found an apartment on 56th

Street, between Fifth and Madison, in one of those narrow Dutch-style houses, which have much charm. On the ground floor is a French restaurant, where they make a delicious *coq au vin*. The apartment is on the third floor, very much smaller than the old one. Also much cozier, much more intimate. She has kept the furniture of the boudoir for the living room, including the sofa upholstered in gold-colored silk.

The bed is new, a large double bed, very low, but the dressing table and the armchair are the old ones. There is not space for more than six or eight dinner guests, but Janet presides over a fairly spacious kitchen and has a pretty room of her own.

I don't know which friends found her this apartment. In Ray's time they saw a lot of people, entertained or were entertained almost every night.

That is a part of her life to which I remain a stranger. As though by common consent, we never mention it. I don't know whom she sees when I'm not in New York, not even if she has one or several lovers.

It's possible. She enjoys making love, without romanticism, I'd almost say without passion, on a friendly basis.

Every time I come, I find her in her dressing gown and I draw her quite naturally toward the sofa on which I had her for the first time. After that, she pours the drinks, takes the two glasses to her bedroom, and starts to dress and make up.

"How is Isabel?"

She never fails to ask after her.

"She still hasn't said anything?"

"She looks at me."

"It's a kind of tactic. . . ."

"What do you mean?"

"If she looks at you long enough without actually saying anything, without any reproaches, she'll make you feel guilty in the end."

"No."

"She relies on that."

"Perhaps, but then she's mistaken."

Mona is puzzled by Isabel, and it is she who is intimidated by her personality. For my part, it is one of the best moments of the day, in fact of the week. She dawdles at her dressing and I plunge blissfully into this intimacy, as into a hot bath. I know every one of her gestures, every face she makes, the way she purses her lips when she puts on her lipstick. When she takes her bath I watch the drops of water that zigzag down her glowing skin. She hasn't Isabel's pink and white complexion; hers is rather a golden color. She is tiny, she weighs next to nothing.

"Has Lowenstein made up his mind?"

For we do discuss her affairs as well. Indeed, they occupy a great deal of our time. Lowenstein is an interior decorator who has made an offer for all the furniture from Sutton Place except for the few pieces Mona has kept.

There was only the question of the price to settle. Now it's done and the lease has been taken by an actress recently arrived from Hollywood for a Broadway engagement.

The arrangements with the Miller brothers are drawing to their conclusion, and the name Sanders has long since been erased from the pane where it followed the names Miller and Miller. There are only a few more details to settle now. I've never asked Mona what she has done with Ray's clothes, with his golf clubs, or with certain personal possessions that I no longer see about the apartment.

Often we go down to lunch in the little ground-floor restaurant and always choose the same corner. The owner comes for a welcoming handshake. We're treated as a couple, and this amuses us.

In the afternoons I usually have to go here and there on Mona's business or sometimes on my own. We arrange to meet in a bar, and drink Martinis, because for our evening drink we have settled on very dry Martinis. We drink a lot, perhaps too much, but without ever getting drunk.

"Where do we go for dinner?"

We just stroll along at random, and sometimes Mona, on her high heels, has to cling to my arm. One day we bumped into Justin Green, from Canaan, one of old Ashbridge's guests, who had been present on that momentous evening. He clearly hesitated whether to greet us. I turned around just as he, too, was turning around, and he seemed embarrassed.

All Brentwood, the whole neighborhood, must now be aware that I am having an "affair" in New York. Did he recognize Mona? It's possible, but not likely, because it was the first time she had been at the Ashbridges', and she hadn't made herself conspicuous.

"A client of yours?"

"A friend of sorts. He lives in Canaan."

"Does it upset you that he has seen us?"

"No."

Quite the contrary, I'd finished with people of that kind. They would come to realize one day that if I still pretended to play the game, I no longer believed in it.

One Saturday I went to Torrington. It's a quiet little town, with only two commercial streets surrounded by residential quarters. To the east there is a small amount of industry, but it is almost of a craftsman type, there is a watch factory and a new tool shop producing minute components for electronic instruments.

The house where I was born is on the main street, at the corner of a dead-end street. "The Citizen," in Gothic Script, is written over the door. Most of the workmen have been with my father for more than thirty years. Everything is ancient, including the machines that filled me with much wonder when I was a child.

It was Saturday, so the offices were closed. But my father was nevertheless in his little glass cage, and one could see him from the street, in his shirt sleeves, as always. This is where he worked, as if to proclaim that his weekly paper had nothing to hide.

The door wasn't locked. I walked in. I sat down at the other side of the desk and waited for my father to raise his head.

"It's you?"

"I'm sorry it's been so long."

"You must have had other things to do, so you needn't apologize."

That was my father's style. I don't believe he ever kissed me, not even when I was a child. All he did at night was hold out his forehead for a peck. I never saw him kiss my mother, either.

"Health all right?"

I replied in the affirmative and at the very same moment noticed how old my father had grown in these last few weeks. His neck was like a chicken's, all string and sinew, and the pupils of his eyes appeared discolored.

"Your wife came by, a day or so ago. . . ."

She had not mentioned it to me.

"She came to do some shopping, to buy some china, I believe, at that old robber Tibbits'."

It was a shop that had been there when I was a child, selling china and silver. I had known old Tibbits, then his son; he was old now, too. Our dinner service, the one we had bought at the time of our marriage, came from Tibbits', and when too many pieces were broken Isabel would come to Torrington to replace them.

"Still content, are you?"

The relationship between my father and me was so restrained that I never knew what meaning to attribute to his questions. He often asked me if I was content in the same way as he asked after Isabel's and our girls' health.

But was there something more to this question? Had

my wife spoken to him? Had he been hearing rumors about me?

He went on scanning the proofs, deleting words which he replaced in the margin by others.

Did we ever really communicate? I sat there, looking at him, now and then turning toward the street which was so much busier now than it had been in my childhood. Once upon a time you could count the number of vehicles and you could park wherever you liked.

"How old are you now?"

"Forty-five."

He shook his head, murmuring as if to himself:

"That's still young . . . considering."

He would be eighty in a few years. He had married late, after his father's death. He had also edited the *Citizen*. His first job had been at Hartford, and for a few months he had worked for a monthly in New York.

I had a brother, Stuart, who in all probability would have gone into the business if he had not been killed in the war. He looked more like my father than I did, and I think they got on very well together.

We did, too, but without intimacy.

"It's your life, after all. . . ."

He mumbled. I needn't have paid any attention. Would it have been better to drop the conversation, to start on another subject?

"You're alluding to Mona?"

My father rearranged his spectacles on his nose and looked at me:

"I didn't know she was called Mona. . . ."

"Isabel didn't tell you?"

"Isabel told me nothing. . . . She's not a woman to talk about her affairs, even to her father-in-law."

There was obvious admiration in his voice. One might have thought that they were of the same breed, he and Isabel.

"Who told you I had a mistress?"

"People talk, word gets around. Apparently she's the widow of your friend Ray."

"That's right."

"The one who had an accident at your place, the night of the blizzard? Isn't that right?"

I blushed because I sensed a vague accusation.

"It's not I who put two and two together, son. It's other people. . . ."

"What people?"

"Your friends from Brentwood, Canaan, Lakeville. Some of them are wondering whether you want to get a divorce and go to live in New York. . . ."

"Certainly not. . . ."

"I'm not putting the question to you, but people have asked me and I've told them it's none of my business. . . ."

He didn't reproach me either. Again like Isabel, he seemed to have no mental reservations. He filled his crooked old pipe and slowly lit it.

"Did you come to tell me something?"

"No. . . ."

"Did you have business in Torrington?"

"No. . . . I just wanted to see you. . . ."

"Would you like to go upstairs?"

He understood that it wasn't just he whom I had come to see, but the house also; that I was here, precisely, to find something of my youth.

It is true that I've always liked to revisit the apartment that was part of the past, where I had crawled before I could stand and where my mother had appeared to me so enormously large. I can still see her unchanging checked apron, which was the fashion at the time.

No. I could no longer go up. Not after what my father had just said.

Neither could I make any contact with him, which I think was what I had wanted.

Why had I come here at all?

"I guess it's a mess up there; Saturdays and Sundays the cleaning woman doesn't come."

I imagined the old man alone in the apartment where the four of us had once lived. He was sucking slowly at his pipe, which emitted a familiar sound.

"Time passes, my boy. . . . It's the same for everybody, you know. You've passed the halfway mark now. . . . I'm beginning to see the end. . . ."

He wasn't pitying himself; it would have been out of character. I felt he was speaking for my benefit, trying to transmit his thoughts to me.

"Isabel was sitting right where you are at the moment. . . . When you introduced her, your mother and I didn't have much to say to her."

I couldn't help smiling. She came from Litchfield, and in the neighborhood the people from Litchfield are considered snobs who believe themselves to be a race apart. Wide avenues, a lot of greenery, lovely, dignified houses, and, especially in the mornings, men and women on horseback. Isabel had had her horse.

"You can be mistaken about people, you see, even when you believe you know them. She is a nice woman."

When my father said about someone that he was nice, it was the greatest compliment he could pay.

"Well, it's your business. . . ."

"I'm not in love with Mona and we have no plans for the future."

He coughed. For several years he had had chronic bronchitis and now and then painful bouts of coughing.

"Excuse me. . . ."

His physical deterioration humiliated him. He hated imposing the sight of it upon others. I believe that is really why he would have preferred us to stop going to see him.

"What's that you were saying? Oh, yes. . . ."

He relit his pipe and, puffing at it, uttered with gaps between the syllables:

"In that case, it's even worse. . . ."

Going to see my father was a mistake. I'm sure I disappointed him. And I, too, had been disappointed. He had not been able to communicate, though, little as he said about it, I gathered he had communicated with Isabel.

When I got into my car, I could see through the window that he was watching me leave, probably thinking, as I did, that perhaps this was to be our last meeting. The whole way home I kept seeing his worn old face, his melancholy dignity, and I wondered about many things. Had he really kept faith until the end, and did he have any illusions left now that he was on the point of going? Did he still believe in the sacred duty of his little weekly paper which, a hundred, even sixty years ago, was a voice in the wilderness crying against injustice, but now served only to flatter people's vanity, with accounts of engagements, marriages, receptions, and all the trivial news items of the neighborhood? He had devoted his life to it as seriously as if it had been a weapon in a battle for some great cause, and he'd cling to it till his last gasp. It would have been the same with my brother if he had not been killed. Had it not, indeed, been the same with me, with some slight differences perhaps, until I lit my first cigarette that night on the bench in the barn?

Lately I have slowed down. These last few days I have suddenly had a feeling of lightheadedness. I'm not ill. Nor is it fatigue, for I'm not working more than I've always done.

Age? It's true that I am aware of my age now, though I never was before, perhaps especially since I've been to see my father.

I wanted to explain to him about Mona; I tried. Would

he have understood that, more than anything else, for me she was a symbol?

We don't love each other. I'm not sure I believe in love, at any rate in love that lasts a lifetime. We come together because it is reassuring to feel the warmth of each other's body, to move in the same rhythm. Making love still provides the closest point of contact between two beings.

We all need somebody. I had needed Isabel, but not in that way. I had needed her as a critic, as a jailer, I don't quite know as what. It is so obsolete now that I myself no longer understand what I looked for in her, and I'm beginning to hate her.

Her eyes exasperate me. It has become an obsession. When I came back, I hadn't mentioned Torrington or my father, but she asked me:

"How is he?"

All right, it was easy enough to guess. There were some clues. But I always feel as though I were at the end of a leash. Wherever I go, whatever I do, somehow it is as though she never took her eyes off me.

Now that the estate is settled I go only once a week to New York, and even with Mona I need an excuse. I mustn't become what I was before, I couldn't bear it. Once one has come to know oneself, in such shattering fashion, it is impossible to go back.

Yes, I need Mona, her presence, that sort of animal intimacy. I like her to sit, naked or half naked, dawdling over make-up and paying no attention to me. I like to feel her skin against mine in bed.

But for the rest, hasn't our experience been a fiasco? I am thinking of the restaurants where we lunch and dine, the little bars where we take our Martinis at the end of the day.

We have remained good friends, no doubt. We have never been embarrassed in front of one another. But to tell the truth, there has been no real communication between us and often I have had to search for a topic of conversation. And she has, too.

Nevertheless she is all that I never had for forty-five years, everything from which I had shied away, in fear.

The girls have come back. I have observed Mildred a lot. I like the color of her skin, like warm bread, and the way in which she wrinkles her nose when she smiles.

She has spent Sunday afternoon with her girl friend, the one who has a brother of twenty. It is what she'll probably later think of as her first love. She doesn't know that the memory of those quick glances, the blushing and the hands that touch as if by accident, will be with her all her life.

She won't be pretty in the usual sense of the word. She isn't handsome, either. What sort of man will she meet and what kind of a life will she have with him?

I can see her as the mother of a family, one of those women I think of as smelling of pastry.

As for Cecilia—I don't know. She remains an enigma and I wouldn't be surprised if she developed into a very strong personality. She scrutinizes us sometimes and I'm almost certain that she doesn't approve of us, that she feels nothing for us but a slight contempt.

It's so strange. For years children are the focal point of all your preoccupations, almost the stimulus of all your activities. The house is organized to suit them, so are Sundays and holidays, and then, one day, you find yourself face to face with them and they are strangers, as my father and I are strangers. I'm convinced now that I was wrong to go to see him. The visit has deepened a pessimism to which I'm only too ready to succumb when I'm not in New York.

And even when I'm there, except for certain occasions that one could count in minutes. It takes very little to start me thinking of conspiracies. Between Isabel and my father, for example. Why did she go to Torrington? Was it vital to replace a few plates, especially as there are only two of us at table now most of the time? It's six months since we've had any guests in the house.

My father says that she didn't speak to him of me or of Mona. It could be, and I have no alternative but to believe him. But didn't he speak about us to her? Even if he hadn't, it would have been enough for them just to look at each other.

"How are things with Donald?"

She must have smiled, a pale smile like the sun after the rain.

"Don't worry about him. . . ."

Wasn't she there to guard me? Doesn't she do that every day, every hour of every day?

Now the local people are involved. They whisper when they see me in the street. At last they have a bit of news to pass on about me. "Donald Dodd, you know, the lawyer whose offices are almost opposite the post office, old Higgins' partner . . . yes, yes, the one who has such a sweet wife, so gentle, so devoted . . . well, he's having an affair in New York!"

Higgins is in it, too. When I tell him that I'll be going to New York tomorrow, he asks:

"You'll stay a couple of days?"

"No, not this time. . . ."

Still, Higgins ought to be satisfied, for the Miller brothers have paid us very substantially for the work I did for them. I'd have done it for nothing, to help Mona. It was they who insisted.

Warren, our doctor, came to see me at my office to ask me about his taxes, as I handle his affairs. He watched me carefully while we were talking and I suspected that this business about taxes was only a pretext.

Isabel was quite capable of telephoning him—of saying to him, for instance:

"Listen, Warren, I'm worried. . . . Donald hasn't been his old self lately. . . . He seems to have changed. He seems odd. . . ."

I suddenly looked him straight in the eyes. He's an old friend. He was at the Ashbridges' on January 15th.

"You, too, find me odd?"

He was so startled he almost dropped his glasses.

"What do you mean?"

"Exactly what I say. . . . People have developed a strange way of turning their heads and whispering when they see me. Isabel looks at me as if she wonders whether I am in my right mind, and I suspect it was she who sent you to see me. . . ."

"I can assure you, Donald . . ."

"Am I odd—yes or no? Do I look like a man in possession of all his faculties?"

"You're joking, surely?"

"Not at all. . . . Do you know that I go to New York to meet a friend with whom I have a sexual relationship?"

I gave an ironical stress to these words.

"Does it surprise you?"

"Why should it surprise me?"

"You knew about it?"

"I'd heard something."

"You see! . . . And what else did they tell you?"

He must have regretted having come, he looked so embarrassed.

"I don't really know. . . . That you might make certain decisions. . . ."

"For instance?"

"To go to live in New York. . . ."

"To get a divorce?"

"Maybe."

"Has Isabel spoken to you about it, too?"

"No. . . ."

"Have you seen her recently?"

"It depends on what you call recently."

"A month ago?"

"I think so. . . ."

"Did she go to see you at your office?"

"You're forgetting about professional etiquette, Donald."

He forced himself to smile and pronounced these words as lightly as he could. He got up, but I wasn't ready yet to let him go.

"If she went to see you, it wasn't on account of her own health. . . . She went to talk to you about me, to tell you she was anxious, that I was no longer myself. . . ."

"I don't like the turn this conversation is taking. . . ."

"Neither do I, but I'm beginning to get tired of being an object of curiosity. . . . I didn't go to see you. You're the one who came here, on a flimsy excuse, to find out what's going on, to take my emotional temperature. . . . Are there any tests you'd like to give me? Have you seen enough to reassure my wife? Do I seem odd to you, too, because I've started telling people the truth? You're Isabel's friend much more than mine. It's the same with all our friends. . . . Isabel is a wonderful woman, so devoted, so kind. . . . Well, my dear Warren, one doesn't go to bed with devotion and kindness. . . . I've done it for too long not to have had enough of it. I'll go to New York or elsewhere, when it suits me, whatever the opinion of my respectable neighbors. As for Isabel, if she is worried you can reassure her. . . . I don't intend to ask for a divorce and I don't intend to start a new life elsewhere. I'll continue working in this office and I'll go back home like a good boy. . . . So—do you still find me odd?"

He shook his head and looked at me sadly.

"I don't know what's eating you, Donald. . . . Have you been drinking?"

"Not yet. . . . But I shall, in a minute."

I was beside myself. I wondered why I had suddenly been overcome with such rage. Especially with poor old Warren, who is certainly the last man I have a grievance against. The pill doctor, as the children call him. On his visits he carries with him a black bag that looks like a traveling salesman's suitcase. It is stuffed with bottles and phials, and after he has examined a patient he looks through his collection, chooses a bottle, tips out two, four, or six pills, as the case may be, which he slips into a little envelope. He has pills of all colors, red, green, and yellow, and even multicolored ones which my daughters, when they were younger, naturally preferred to all the others.

"There you are. . . . Take one a quarter of an hour before dinner and another before retiring. . . . The same tomorrow morning. . . ."

Poor Warren! I had shaken him and my anger was going as quickly as it had come.

"Please forgive me, old boy. . . . If you were in my place, you'd understand. . . . As for my mental state, I don't think you need worry yet. . . . Do you agree?"

"I never thought for a moment . . ."

"Possibly not, but others have been thinking it. . . . You can reassure Isabel. But don't tell her I told you."

"So you're not angry with me?"

"Not in the least."

I wasn't angry with him, but I was disturbed, because I was asking myself whether I hadn't just discovered the reason for the anxiety in my wife's eyes.

She had always been so sure of me, so sure of what she must have considered to be my sense of balance, that she couldn't conceive that I might deliberately change.

I always came back to the cigarette butts she had removed. Was it possible that she believed I had pushed Ray?

My trips to New York, my intimacy with Mona, almost cynically flaunted immediately after my friend's death—might they not constitute a proof in her eyes?

If so, I must simply be out of my mind. It was the only key to my attitude. . . .

I had just mentioned drinking, and I actually crossed the road and had a Scotch in the bar opposite, frequented mainly by truckdrivers, a place I hardly ever entered.

"Another one. . . ."

Here they were gaping at me, too, of course, and if Lieutenant Olsen had come in, my presence would have given him something to think about.

There's another one who had his doubts. I'm surprised that he hadn't been sniffing around again. Was he convinced that Ray's death was accidental? He must have heard the rumors that I was Mona's lover and that we were seen in New York strolling about hand in hand.

I didn't have a third Scotch, much as I wanted it. I crossed the street and went back to the office.

"Are you going to New York this week?"

"Why do you ask?"

"Because, if you are going, you might do something for me. . . . What part of town will you be staying in?"

"On 56th Street. . . ."

"It's about a document that has to be registered at the Belgian Consulate, Rockefeller Center."

"I may go on Thursday."

"You certainly shattered poor Warren just now. . . . I tried hard, but I couldn't help overhearing."

"You find me odd, too?"

"Odd, no. But you have changed. To the point that I've asked myself if you'll be staying here and if I'd have to go and look for another partner. A nice mess I'd be in. . . . Can you see me, at my age, breaking in a young man? Did the Millers make you an offer?"

"No. . . ."

"That surprises me. . . ."

I wasn't telling the truth. They hadn't made me a direct offer, that was correct. But they questioned me about my plans, my life at Brentwood, and I could see what they were driving at.

They, too, were wrong when it came to my relations with Mona. They believed in a passionate love affair and imagined that in a few weeks I would settle in New York to live with her and marry her.

If I'd done that, I really would have stepped into Ray's shoes!

"In any case, I'm glad you're staying. . . ."

From his office overlooking the street he had seen me cross over and walk into the bar opposite, which isn't one of my habits.

What does he think, the old fox, who looks more like a crafty cattle dealer than a lawyer? What does it matter, anyway? Let them think what they like, all of them. Isabel included, in fact, Isabel first and foremost!

When I got back she welcomed me with a sickly smile, as if I were a poor wretch, or ill.

It's a game that I begin to find hard to bear, and I'll have to get used to it. I must resolve once and for all to pay no attention to the way she looks at me. It's a game she plays on purpose. It is her secret weapon, and she knows that I try to understand, that it makes me feel uneasy, that it saps my self-assurance.

She has a whole set of kicks, which she uses like precision instruments. Words I might have dealt with, but there's nothing one can do about eyes.

If I asked her: "Why do you look at me like that?" she would reply by another question:

"How am I looking at you?"

In all sorts of ways. The expression changes with the days, with the hours. Sometimes the eyes are vacant, and that is perhaps most disturbing of all. She's there. We eat. I say a few words to avoid a painful silence. And she looks at me with eyes that are blank. She looks at my lips moving, as one watches the mouth of a fish open and shut in a bowl.

But then at other times her eyes narrow and she stares at me as though she were asking herself some distressing question. What question? Are there any left after seventeen years of marriage?

Her attitudes, her way of standing, her habit of tilting her head slightly to one side, the flicker of a smile, all these have never changed, have remained constant; as if she were a statue.

Unfortunately, the statue was my wife and she had eyes.

The strangest feeling of all was when I bent down, morning and evening, to touch her forehead or her cheek with my lips. She didn't move, there wasn't the slightest physical reaction.

"Good morning, Isabel."

"Good morning, Donald."

I might just as well have been slipping a dime into the collection box, in church. I tried not to undress in front of her. It embarrassed me as it embarrassed me to see her half naked. Yet she continued to do it. She did it on purpose. Not with impropriety. She had always been a great prude. But as an acquired right. There were only two people in the world in front of whom she had the right to undress: her husband and her doctor.

Had Warren called her, after our brief exchange? Had he reassured her? Had he told her what had happened?

There were moments when I wanted to explode, like that morning at my office. But I controlled myself. I didn't want to give her that satisfaction. For it would undoubtedly have given her satisfaction.

Not only was she intelligent, kind, devoted, indulgent —what else? But in that way I would have also supplied her with the crown of a martyr.

I really hated her. And I realized that it wasn't altogether her fault. Nor mine, either. She represented all the agony I had suffered, the wet-blanketing of my entire life, the humiliation that I had imposed upon myself.

"Don't pick your nose."

"Old people must be treated with respect."

"Go and wash your hands, Donald."

"Take your elbows off the table."

These were not Isabel's phrases. They came from my mother. But for seventeen years Isabel's expression had said exactly the same thing to me.

I know that I had only myself to blame because I had chosen her.

And the most ridiculous thing of all was that I had chosen her for that very purpose.

To watch over me? To be my judge? To prevent me from doing too many stupid things? It's possible. It is hard for me to remember what my state of mind was when I met her. At that time I was debating whether or not to join Ray in New York. Somebody had spoken of a job in Los Angeles and I had been tempted.

What could I have become? What would I have become, without Isabel?

Would I have married someone like Mona?

Would I, like Ray, have made a lot of money and ended by despising myself to the point of talking about suicide?

I don't know. I prefer not to know, to ask myself no more questions. I would like to have established a very clear, a very orderly dossier, without any gaps. I'm a long way from that. For at my age I am still wary of the expression in my wife's eyes!

II

The spring vacation was very painful. The weather was glorious, with the same gentle sunshine every day, and there were a few golden clouds in the sky. The rock garden under the windows of the living room was bright with flowers and buzzing with bees.

In spite of the cool weather, the girls bathed in the swimming pool, and Isabel went in with them once or twice. We made a trip to Cape Cod, where we walked for hours barefoot on the beach, next to an almost foamless sea.

In my inmost self, I felt neither a husband nor a father. I was no longer anything. An empty shell. An automaton. Even my legal work no longer interested me and I saw too clearly the duplicity of my clients. I was no better than they were. I had done nothing to prevent Ray from dying in the snow at the foot of the rock. The question wasn't whether I might have been able to change what had happened. Baldly stated, the fact was that I had gone and sat down on the red bench in the barn.

And little by little, smoking cigarettes in my refuge

from the blizzard, I had felt an almost physical satisfaction, a warm sensation in the chest, at the idea that he was dead or in the process of dying.

That night I had discovered that during all the time I had known him, I had never ceased to envy him and to dislike him.

I hadn't been a friend, and neither was I a husband, a father, a citizen, or any of the other parts I had played. It had all been a mask. The Scriptures' whited sepulcher.

What remained?

All through the Easter weekend when I couldn't escape, Isabel watched me with more alertness than ever.

It was as if my discomfort delighted her. She didn't dream of helping me. Rather, she seemed to be scheming diabolically to squash me for good. For instance, I tried several times to start a conversation with Mildred. She is reaching the age when you can talk about serious things with her. Every time, Isabel's expression paralyzed me, seeming to say:

"Poor Donald! . . . Can't you see that these attempts are hopeless, that your daughters are quite out of touch with you?"

We had been close when they were small. They'd come to me sooner than to their mother.

What image do they have of me nowadays?

I'm no longer of any importance. When my advice is asked, my reply is not listened to. I'm the gentleman who spends his days in the office to earn the required money, a gentleman who is getting on in years, whose features are beginning to sharpen, who no longer knows how to laugh or to play.

Does Isabel realize the danger she's provoking? It's possible. I admit I no longer know. I begin to be exasperated, trying to interpret her every look, watching her eyes fixed on me.

She is lively with the children, full of initiative. Every morning she finds something pleasant to fill their day. Pleasant for her and for the two girls, of course. We've gone on several hikes, twice into the hills. I have a horror of hikes and picnics, of long marches in Indian file during which you automatically pluck at the wild flowers at the side of the road.

Isabel is radiant. At least when she is talking to the girls. The moment she looks at me, or speaks to me—down come the shutters again. Is she trying to push me to the limits of my endurance? Sometimes it seems she wants to push me to the edge and then, perhaps, she will stretch out her hand to me and murmur:

"Poor Donald."

I'm not poor Donald, I'm a man, a complete man, but this she'll never recognize.

The children must have been conscious of the tension. I felt a certain suspicion, a certain sense of reproach between them and me, especially when I poured myself a drink.

Now, as if by chance, every time I suggest a Scotch to Isabel she replies primly:

"No, thank you."

I'm forced to drink alone. I haven't had too much a single time. There has never been any change in my behavior. No trouble with speech, no excitement.

Nevertheless my daughters look at me when I have a glass in my hand as though I were committing a sin.

It's something quite new. They have often seen us having a drink or two, their mother and me. Has Isabel said something to them?

There exists between them a certain complicity just as there is between Isabel and my father. She has the gift of eliciting sympathy and admiration, as well as confidence.

She is so kind, so understanding.

She'd better watch out, because one of these days I shall have had enough. I've worked out a line of conduct for myself—I stick to it, but I'm beginning to grit my teeth.

I didn't take the girls back to Litchfield, but left that duty to my wife. On purpose. In order to give her the opportunity of putting them in the picture in whatever way she felt inclined. As an act of defiance, in fact.

"Don't pay any attention to your father's eccentricities, my darlings. . . . He's going through a bad spell. . . . Ray's accident has shaken him a lot and his nerves are not what they ought to be. . . ."

"Why does he drink, Mummy?"

She could have answered that I don't drink any more

than any other friend of ours. But she certainly wouldn't do that.

"It's purely and simply nerves . . . to give himself confidence."

"Sometimes he looks at us as though he hardly knew us. . . ."

"I know. . . . He shuts himself away. . . . I've talked about it to Dr. Warren, and he has been to see him. . . ."

"Is Dad ill?"

"It isn't really an illness. It's in his mind. . . . He imagines things. . . ."

"What you call neurasthenia?"

"Perhaps. . . . It looks like it. . . . It often happens at his age. . . ."

Is that the way they talk about me, the three of them? I swear it is. I can almost hear them. And Isabel's gentle, tolerant voice, her candid expression turned toward the children. How reassuring it is to be looked at like that! You get the impression that you're looking into a fountain of freshness and generosity unpolluted throughout the years.

The whole thing is maddening! In the office, my secretary is also beginning to observe me anxiously. If this continues, everybody will be feeling sorry for me.

Sorry or afraid?

I can feel Higgins' perplexity. For that old rogue, life is simple, it's each man for himself. Anything goes, as long as you keep inside the law. And there exist a thousand legitimate ways of bending the law to your purpose. It's his profession. He practices it with a calm effrontery, without the slightest pangs of conscience.

Lieutenant Olsen passed me as I was going to the post office and raised his hand in a vague greeting as he drove by in the police car. Is he still wondering about Ray? These people, once they get a notion in their heads . . .

Well, I've done it at last! I telephoned Mona from the office, quite boldly. My secretary and even Higgins could hear what I said, because we always leave the doors open unless one of us is with a client.

At first as the telephone went on ringing I was afraid she might not have returned from Long Island, where she had gone to spend a few days with some friends who have a place out there, and horses and a yacht. I don't know them. She didn't tell me their name and I didn't ask her.

They had many friends, she and Ray. She had a great many even before she met Ray. Often, when we stroll in the streets, people greet her more or less familiarly, some just throwing out a "Hello, Mona" as they pass. . . . Since I'm with her, I mutter something in return and ask no questions. Often she will just say, as if it explained everything:

"That was Harris."

Or:

"That was Helen."

Harris who? Helen who? Probably well-known people

in the theater, or the movies, or television. Ray was working on television accounts at the Millers'. It had become his specialty, and it was probably the reason why he had asked his wife not to act any more on the screen. He might have found himself in an awkward situation.

But now? Wouldn't Mona want to go back to work again? She didn't talk to me about it. There is no common ground between us there. There is quite a large part of her life that is a closed book to me.

"Hello, Mona. . . . Yes, it's Donald."

"How did it go?"

"Badly. And you? On Long Island?"

"I'm a bit worn out. . . . I didn't have a moment to myself. . . . Crowds of people, as many as twenty at a time."

"Did you ride?"

"I even was thrown, but luckily I didn't hurt myself."

"Did you go sailing?"

"Twice. . . . I've got a fine tan. . . ."

"Are you free tomorrow?"

"Wait. . . . What day is it?"

"Wednesday."

"Eleven o'clock?"

"I'll be with you at eleven."

It was our time, the time when she dressed, the time that I enjoyed most of all with a marvelous feeling of intimacy and complete abandon.

The next day the sky was still clear, a lavender blue

with golden clouds above the hills, which seemed to be arrested there forever as in a picture. Only on a few rare nights these clouds disappear or extend in long, crimson ribbons across the sky.

I drove off gaily.

"You'll be back tonight?"

"Probably. . . ."

Does Isabel ask herself why I have recently stayed less often in New York overnight? Does she imagine that something has changed between Mona and me? Or that I'm beginning to get a grip on myself, to avoid compromising myself any further?

"I hate her!"

I looked a long time for a parking space before going into the house on 56th Street. I rushed to the elevator. I rang. The door opened immediately and I saw Mona standing there dressed in a light emerald-green suit, with a little white hat tilted over the left ear.

I was stunned. She was surprised, as if she hadn't expected she would produce that effect.

"My poor Donald . . ."

I don't like being poor Donald, even for her. I couldn't take her in my arms the way I did when she received me in her dressing gown.

"Are you disappointed?"

We kissed, all the same. It was true, her face was tanned, and that helped to make her look different.

"I wanted to take a walk with you in Central Park this morning. . . . Do you mind?"

My face lit up. It was a charming idea. The weather was perfect. We hadn't celebrated spring together before.

"Would you like a drink before we go?"

"No. . . ."

She turned toward the kitchen.

"I won't be back for lunch, Janet. . . ."

"Very well, Madam."

"If anyone calls, I'll be back around two or three o'clock."

It wasn't the first time that we'd strolled along the sidewalks, but the air was brisker than usual, the sunshine was gay and the sky surprisingly light and clear between the skyscrapers.

As we passed the Plaza Hotel, we saw the few carriages that always stand there waiting for tourists or lovers. For a moment it occurred to me to take one of them. Mona was paying no attention. Her hand lay lightly on my arm.

"How are Mildred and Cecilia?"

"Very well. They spent the holidays with us. We made several trips together . . . even as far as Cape Cod."

We proceeded slowly toward the pond, where we used to skate sometimes in winter, Ray and I, when we were students and had a night out in New York.

I felt a stronger pressure on my arm from the hand in its white glove.

"I've got to talk to you, Donald. . . ."

It was queer. I felt a sudden chill, not in my body but

in my head, and I said in a voice that I barely recognized:

"What is it?"

"We're old friends, you and I, aren't we? You're the best friend I've ever had. . . ."

There were mothers watching their children walking unsteadily and a derelict beggar sleeping on a bench, looking so utterly wretched that I had to look away.

We walked slowly. I studied the gravel under my feet.

"Do you know John Falk?"

I had read his name somewhere. It seemed familiar, but for the moment I couldn't place him. I didn't try. I was waiting for the sentence. For all this was leading to a sentence—inevitably.

"He's the producer of the three best serials on C.B.S."

I had nothing to say. I could hear the noises of the park, the birds, the children's voices, the traffic on Fifth Avenue. I could see the ducks preening themselves on the grass, others swimming on the water leaving a triangular wake behind them.

"We've known each other for a long time, he and I. He is forty. He's been divorced for three years and has a little girl."

She added very quickly, as though it had to be said:

"We're planning to get married, Donald. . . ."

I said nothing. I couldn't have said anything.

"Are you sad?"

I almost laughed, the word was so ridiculous. Sad?

I was stunned. . . . I was . . . I can't explain it. . . . There was simply nothing left, that was all. . . .

Up till now I had had something, I had had Mona even if our affair was limited, even if there was no question of love between us. . . .

I could see the boudoir, the movement of her lips toward the lipstick, the dressing gown that she let trail behind her. . . .

"Forgive me. . . ."

"For what?"

"For hurting you. . . . I know I'm hurting you. . . ."

"A little," I said at last, and I too used a ridiculously inadequate word.

"I should have said something to you before. . . . I've been wondering what to do for a month now. . . . I didn't know what was best. . . . I even thought of having you meet John and asking your advice. . . ."

We were not looking at each other. She had thought it all out. That's why she had taken me to the park. Walking among other people, there's no question of a scene.

"When are you planning . . . ?"

"Oh, not for some time. . . . There are various legal matters holding things up. . . . And then we have to find another apartment, because Monique will live with us. . . ."

So the little girl's name was Monique.

"Her father has the custody. . . . He simply adores her."

Of course! Of course! And meanwhile, this John Falk, has he already slept in the large double bed on 56th Street?

It was probable. On a friendly basis, as Mona says. No, theirs was not on a friendly basis; they were going to marry.

"I'm desperately sorry, Donald. . . . We can still be friends, can't we?"

And then?

"I told John about you."

"Did you tell him the truth?"

"Why not? He doesn't think I'm a virgin. . . ."

The word shocked me, spoken like that, suddenly, in the middle of the sunlit park.

I'm not in love with Mona, I swear it. Nobody'll believe me, but it's the truth. It's not just that, for me, she was a woman—it's . . . everything, yes! And at the same time, nothing! If she could break off so easily, then I had to believe it was nothing.

She was going back to television. I would see her on the screen, sitting in the library at Brentwood next to Isabel.

"I thought we might lunch together, wherever you'd like."

"He's the call you're expecting between two and three o'clock?"

"Yes. . . ."

"He knows you're with me?"

"Yes. . . ."

"He knows you've taken me to Central Park?"

"No. . . . I thought of it as I was dressing."

Not as she was dressing in front of me, with her marvelous relaxed lack of modesty. Dressing alone. Or perhaps with Janet there.

"It's going to be hard, Janet."

"He'll understand, Madam. . . ."

"Of course he'll understand, but I'm going to hurt him, all the same. . . ."

"If one had to give up everything that makes other people suffer . . ."

Mona lit a cigarette and looked at me out of the corner of her eye, and I smiled at her. At least it was supposed to be a smile.

"You'll come and see me?"

"I don't know."

I wouldn't. I had nothing in common with Mr. and Mrs. Falk. Or with a little girl called Monique.

I had two girls of my own, my daughters.

It seemed as if the sun was suddenly stronger than it had been before. We walked into the bar of the Plaza.

"Two double Martinis."

I didn't ask her what she wanted. Perhaps she had another kind of drink with Falk. I kept to our tradition for the last time.

"To you, Donald."

"To you, Mona."

That was the hardest of all. When I spoke her name, stupidly I almost burst into tears. Those two syllables . . .

Why should one try to explain? I could see myself in the mirror between the bottles.

"Where would you like to lunch?"

She left the choice to me. It was my day. My last day. So it was important that everything should go well.

"We can go to our little French restaurant."

I shook my head. No, I preferred a crowd, a place without memories.

We lunched at the Plaza; the big room was packed. I suggested some *foie gras* almost ironically and she accepted. Then lobster. It was a gala luncheon!

"Would you like some *crêpes Suzette*?"

"Why not?"

She believed she was giving me pleasure by accepting. I could see her glance now and then at the clock. I bore her no grudge. She had given me what she was able to give, very sweetly, a warm animal tenderness, and it was I who was in her debt. At one moment I saw her hand flat on the tablecloth just as I had seen it on the floor, that January night, and the same desire moved me to seize the hand.

"Courage, Donald."

She could guess what was happening.

"If you only knew how it hurts me . . ." she sighed.

Then we walked back to her house. I was longing to suggest:

"Couldn't we . . . ? One last time?"

I felt it would be easier, afterward. I looked up at the windows of the third floor. We stepped into the hall.

"*Au revoir,* Donald."

"Good-by, Mona."

She threw herself into my arms and, oblivious of her make-up, gave me a long, deep kiss.

"I'll never forget . . ." she gasped.

Then very quickly, almost feverishly, she opened the door of the elevator.

III

A month has gone by, and my hatred of Isabel has only increased. As I might have known, she understood at once when she saw me come back. I wasn't even drunk. I had felt no need of liquor.

As I drove my car along the Taconic Parkway I drew a picture in my mind of the life that I would be leading from now on from morning till night—the comings and goings from one room to another, the morning mail, the office, the secretary who was on the point of leaving, luncheon, clients, the letters, the Scotch before dinner, dinner with Isabel, television, a newspaper and a book . . . I left nothing out. On the contrary, I sketched in all the details as with pen and ink.

It was an engraving, an album of engravings—a day in the life of a man called Donald Dodd.

Isabel said nothing; I knew she wouldn't. I could tell, too, that she felt no pity, nor would I have liked her to feel any. She succeeded, however, in hiding her triumph, in keeping her eyes as tranquil as ever.

Then, on the following days, she began again to observe me, as one observes a sick man, wondering whether he will live or die.

I wasn't dying. The physical mechanics functioned perfectly smoothly. I was well trained. My gestures were the same, as were the words I uttered, my behavior at table, in the office, in the evening in my easy chair.

Why was she still watching me? What was she hoping for?

She wasn't satisfied, I sensed it. She needed something else. My complete annihilation, perhaps? I had no intention of destroying myself.

Next week Higgins was surprised not to see me go to New York. So was my secretary.

The week after, he was relieved, no doubt having gathered that what he called my "affair" had come to an end. So I was going to return to the world of decent people, of normalcy. I had had a kind of moral influenza and was quietly recovering.

He tried to be nice to me, to be encouraging, came several times a day into my office to talk about business, which, normally, he would only have referred to in passing.

Surely now I would take a renewed interest in life!

I met Warren, too, at the post office, where many people come to collect their morning mail. Remembering the welcome I had given him the last time, he hesitated to approach me, but then ended by doing just that.

"You look well, Donald."

But of course I do!

I avoided going to New York, even when it would have been a good idea, trying to settle everything by telephone or letter. One day when my presence was called for I asked Higgins to go in my place, and he agreed immediately.

It meant that I had recovered, or almost recovered.

If they could have known, all of them, how I hated her! But she was the only one to know that.

For I had finally understood. For a long time I had searched for the meaning of her look. I had made surmise after surmise without coming to the simple truth. I had detached myself from her. I had broken the circle. I was no longer within her reach. That she could never forgive. I was her property, like the house, the girls, like Brentwood and our everyday life.

I had escaped and was looking at her from outside, I looked at her with hatred because she had owned me for too much of my life, because she had stifled me, because she had prevented me from living.

Very well, I had chosen her. I admitted it to myself and I kept saying it, but it altered nothing. It didn't keep me from making her, here, beside me, in the bed next to mine, the sum total of all that I had begun to hate.

I couldn't blame the whole world and all its institutions. I couldn't spit out their half-truths and mine into the faces of millions of human beings.

She was there.

Just as, at one time, Mona had been there and, as far as she could, had represented life.

All that Isabel knew. The qualities that others credited her with may or may not have existed, but there was one talent she had to a very high degree: the talent to forage in other people's psyches and in particular in mine.

Now she was having the time of her life; she searched all day, sensing that there was nothing left but a façade and that when that cracked—there would be nothing!

To see me reduced to zero—what a marvelous sensation that would be! What an unprecedented vengeance!

"Isabel deserves a lot of credit."

To have lived with such a man, obviously. To have suffered all that she had had to suffer these last months.

"He made no effort to conceal it. . . ."

At night I found it more and more difficult to go to sleep, and after an hour of immobility I would go to the bathroom and swallow a sleeping pill. She knew it. I'm certain that she tried not to fall asleep before I did, so as to enjoy my insomnia, to listen to the mysterious rustle of my thoughts.

It wasn't so much Mona's face that haunted me, and I'm not sure that Isabel found that out. It was the bench. The red bench. The din of the storm and of the door that banged back and forth in a regular rhythm, the snow that every moment pushed farther and farther into the barn.

It was Ray, with Patricia, in the bathroom. I would

have given everything to have been in his place. I wanted Patricia. Someday when the Ashbridges return from Florida . . .

Ray was dead. His apartment on Sutton Place, which had cost him so much and the blatant luxury of which he had exhibited so ironically, had been dismantled and was occupied by a movie actress.

His wife Mona would be Mrs. Falk. He had been a friend of his. A producer with whom Ray had done business.

He had contemplated suicide, and death had come to him without his having to make a single move in its direction. . . .

The lucky man!

My father went on publishing his *Citizen,* writing articles which were read by two or three dozen old men. Had Isabel told him that the affair with Mona was finished? Was he assuming, as did the others, that finally I was back on the straight and narrow path?

I couldn't stand her eyes any longer. It got to the point that I had to turn away. Already I had eliminated the peck on the forehead and on the cheek, morning and evening. She had made no remark about that. I may be mistaken, but it seemed to me that there was a slight glimmer of hope in her eyes.

If that was the way I reacted, didn't it mean that I was affected in some way? Had I been indifferent, I could have continued the old routine without minding it, without noticing it.

It was almost a declaration of war. I had become an enemy, an enemy who lived in the house, beside her, ate at the same table, slept in the same room.

The month of May began gloriously with days as hot as summer. I already wore my cotton suit, my straw hat. In the office, the air-conditioning was on. In the morning, before going to work, I plunged into the swimming pool and did the same when I got home in the evening.

Isabel had chosen a different time to swim, for she was never in the water when I was there, not a single time.

"You've got a lot of work?"

"Enough to fill my time and pay our bills."

The house was ours and was worth about sixty thousand dollars. I had insured myself, many years ago, for a hundred thousand dollars, which had seemed enormous to me at the time, for I was only starting out then.

Every year I bought some shares of stock.

If I were to go away, alone, without saying a word, to disappear in the anonymous swarm, neither my wife nor my daughters would have found themselves in any difficulties.

But where was I to go? Sometimes at night, in my bed, I would think of the man in Central Park, the one who at midday slept on a bench, his mouth open, within sight of all the passers-by.

He needed no one. Nor did he need to pretend. He wasn't concerned with the opinions of other men, with the proprieties, with what can or can't be done. And when the police picked him up, he could go on sleeping in jail.

I wasn't obliged to do anything as drastic as that. I could have . . .

But then, why do anything? I had already escaped on the spot, in a way. The puppet still worked, but I had cut the strings and nobody pulled them any longer.

Except Isabel. She was there, lying on her back in bed, silent, listening to my breathing, trying to discover what my phantoms were. She was waiting for the moment when, unable to stand it any longer, I'd get up to go and take my two sleeping pills. I had to have two, now. Soon I would need three. Was this more serious than drink?

I had been tempted to drink. Often I would glance at the liquor cupboard, longing to snatch the first bottle I laid my hands on and to drink straight from it as the man in Central Park would have done.

What was she really waiting for? Was she waiting for me suddenly to roar out in a fit of fury? Or of pain? Or what?

But I didn't roar, and then she would provoke me. When I got up to take my sleeping pills, she would sometimes ask, quite gently, the way one speaks to a child or an invalid:

"You're not sleeping, Donald?"

She could see I wasn't sleeping, couldn't she? I wasn't a sleepwalker. Then why ask?

"Perhaps you should go and see Dr. Warren. . . ."

Of course, of course! She was trying to persuade me that I was sick. She must have persuaded other people of it, too.

"He's going through a bad spell. . . . I don't know why. . . . Dr. Warren can't make head or tail of it. . . . He thinks it's his morale."

The man whose morale is not what it should be . . . I could see the whole thing, what people were thinking, the commiserating looks. Before, I had been the man who had a mistress and who might get a divorce any day. Now I was the husband who was going through a bad spell.

"Only yesterday I bumped into him in the street and he didn't recognize me. . . ."

As though I would take the trouble to identify every character I met in the street!

She is a vicious woman. I'm not the one who is collecting a dossier. It's Isabel. Patiently, with gentle little touches here and there, the way one weaves a tapestry. Strangely enough, she's actually weaving one now. Two chairs in the living room are covered with tapestry woven by Isabel.

She weaves . . . she weaves. . . .

And looks at me fiercely, waiting for me to crack.

Isn't she frightened yet?

IV

I'm quite calm, in a lucid state of mind that I believe few men ever attain. This isn't a speech for the defense. I'm not trying to exonerate myself, I'm not writing it for anyone in particular.

It is three o'clock in the morning. It is May 27th and the day has been stifling. Nothing particular happened. I had a lot of work in the office and did it conscientiously. I know now that our secretary is pregnant but that after a few months off she intends to come back to work.

It has no more importance for me, now; it will be Higgins' business.

Last night as soon as I got into bed I found that it felt damp, because the rooms are not air-conditioned. The complicated layout of the house makes air-conditioning almost impossible.

At half past twelve I couldn't sleep, and I went to take my two pills.

She didn't speak to me but her eyes followed me. She literally picked me up at the moment I was leaving the bed, watched me walk toward the bathroom, and when I left it I found her eyes waiting to bring me back.

Sleep didn't come. The drug has lost its effect. I don't dare increase the dose without Warren's advice, and I don't particularly want to see Warren at the moment.

Like me, she was lying on her back. My eyes were open, for it is even harder when I close them and there is only the noise of my heart to listen to.

I could, if I pricked up my ears, hear hers.

Two hours passed. It's incredible the number of images that can flash past in the mind in two hours. I kept seeing the hand on the floor of the living room. I wonder why this hand has acquired such importance for me? I've held the whole body in my arms, and I know it in all its smallest details, in every kind of light. But still, it's the hand that sticks in my memory, the hand lying on the floor near my mattress. I switched on the light over the bed, got out of bed, and went to the bathroom.

"Aren't you feeling well, Donald?"

Because I'm not in the habit of getting up twice. I swallowed another pill, and then another, to put an end to the insomnia. When I came back to the room she was sitting up in bed looking at me.

Hadn't she just about reached her goal? Hadn't she just heard the first crack?

I had no time to think. The gesture was spontaneous and I was perfectly calm. I opened the bedside-table drawer, between our beds, and seized the revolver.

She was still looking at me, without a frown, without a shadow in her eyes. She was still defying me.

Was not my first idea perhaps to turn the weapon against myself, as Ray had been tempted to do?

It's probable, but I couldn't swear to it.

She looked at the barrel, then at me. One thing I'm sure of, and that is that a smile flickered across her face and that there was a light of triumph in her blue eyes.

I pulled the trigger, aiming at the chest, and felt no emotion at all. The eyes were still fixed on me, motionless. Then I fired two more shots.

Into those eyes.

I'm going to telephone Lieutenant Olsen to tell him what has happened. They'll talk of unhinged sexuality and involve Mona, who has nothing to do with it at all.

I'll be examined by a psychiatrist.

What difference can prison make to me when I've been in prison all my life?

I've just called Olsen. He didn't seem very surprised. He said:

"I'll be right there. . . ."

And then he added:

"Whatever happens, don't do anything foolish. . . ."

Epalinges, April 29, 1968